Caffeine Night

Glory Boys 2

Days of Change

Jim Iron & John Steel

Fiction aimed at the heart
and the head..

Published by Caffeine Nights Publishing 2022

CONDITIONS OF SALE

Published in Great Britain by
Caffeine Nights Publishing
71 Buckthorne Road
Thistle Hill
Minster on Sea
Isle of Sheppey
ME12 3RD
caffeinenightsbooks com

Also available as an eBook

British Library Cataloguing in Publication Data.
A CIP catalogue record for this book is available from the British Library

ISBN: 978-1-913200-22-0

Everything else by
Default, Luck and Accident

For Tracey and Dave. And for I, P, F and W.

The authors would like to thank Tom, Grant, Barney, Dave and the East London Glory Boys of 1979.

Special thanks to Secret Affair for Behind Closed Doors – a lasting inspiration.

Glory Boys 2
Days of Change

1

Friday 18th of April, 1980.

'Gonna have fun in the city/ Be with my girl, she's so pretty/ She looks fine tonight/ She is out of sight to me...' With The Easybeats' 'Friday On My Mind' buzzing around his head, Chris Davis rammed the empty mail trolley hard against the wall. CLUNK! The echo of metal hitting concrete had barely faded in the underground bunker that passed for a workplace when a small angry Scottish voice parped up.

'Hey, Davis, watch what you're doing for fuck's sake,' squealed Alec Norton. 'That is Shell company property, laddie.'

'Dick,' thought Chris. He ignored his 'superior' and walked on to his locker. Chris hated Norton, he was a puffed-up little creep, full of his own imagined importance. And the feeling was entirely mutual. Normally new mailroom staff at the Shell Centre were eventually ground down by Norton's endless badgering. But after more than a whole year in the soul-sapping job, Chris would still not acknowledge the odious little jug-nosed bastard's overblown sense of authority. To him, the twat was just living proof that Loch Ness had lost its dullest monster.

Chris did his work well though, and those higher up the tree liked him, so Norton just had to accept it and fester away, like... Chris searched for a suitable simile... yeah, like a little white dog turd slowly rotting on a hot pavement. He made himself smile with that.

'I've got your annual review pencilled in for next week lad,' the Balloch-born, bollocks-spouting buffoon continued impotently. 'You'd better be in here next week and ready to impress. I've got a few notes in my diary that need addressing. Timekeeping, attitude, efficiency… there's plenty to discuss, so…' Norton's sentence faded away like steam from a cooling kettle as even he seemed to realise that he was pissing against the wind.

'Yeah, yeah, see you, Jimmy,' thought Chris as he blanked his boss again. 'See you next Tuesday – cunt.' He had often thought about giving Norton a review of his own, up against the wall with a pair of fucking knuckle-dusters. But he could wait. Chris glanced at his watch, grunted and strode towards the heavy swing doors that took him out of the airless hell of the mailroom and that little bit closer to freedom. It was Friday, four o'clock and his whole body tingled with possibilities.

This is my weekend, he thought, my world, and that haggis-munching, pencil-dicked cowson could fuck right off until Monday morning… if he even made it back to work by then. Anything was possible.

5-4-3-2-1. Blast off!

'Tonight, I'll spend my bread, tonight I'll lose my head, tonight, I've got to get to night…'

To the untrained eye, Chris Davis already looked sharp, but that was work smart. Friday nights at the Barge Aground in less-than-beautiful downtown Barking required an altogether more sussed degree of sartorial sharpness. Along with the Bridge House in Canning Town, The Wellington at Waterloo, and The Bedford's Head in Covent Garden, the Barge had become the focal point of the Mod scene. It was definitely the place to be on the London circuit most weekends, unless there was something really special happening elsewhere. It attracted a good mix of Mods and a smattering of cooler skinheads – more like suede-heads really – who disliked the way punk was dragging many of their dimmer brethren into the scruffier realm of the glue-sniffing bonehead.

The dawning of a new decade had thinned Mod numbers down slightly but with the bandwagon jumpers and fly-by-night fashion whores out of the way, everyone still standing was there for all the right reasons.

As Chris cut through the traffic on the Belvedere Road on his Vespa, he could feel the anticipation building already. His PX 125 was gleaming white and buffed to within an inch of its life. It featured a custom seat, a few mirrors and a backrest with a white-walled spare tyre strapped to it. Some Mods went well overboard on the customisation front but Chris liked his wheels to be clean, sharp and stylish – just like him. It cost a few bob, but fuck it, that's what he grafted for.

Working at the Shell Centre on London's Southbank was a grind, but it paid well and it fed his unceasing desire for good clobber and endless speed-fuelled socialising. The rise he had received after his first full year there had also allowed him to get his own flat. In reality it was no more than a bedsit close to his parents' drum in Morgan Street, but it was his space and the independence allowed him to spend more time with Charlotte without his old man leering at her or his mother earwigging whenever they tried to have a furtive bunk-up.

The cramped flat had literally brought them closer together as well. At the start it was blissful. Charlotte had almost moved in at one point, but that was before her life took a massive change of direction. One Sunday they had been stopped in the street in Soho by a well-dressed old bird who blurted out that Charlotte 'simply must' consider modelling and jammed a business card into her hand before swishing off into the Lyric boozer. Chris was initially suspicious and suspected that the woman was either a dyke or an old madam looking to turn his stunningly attractive girlfriend into a top-class brass but Charlotte's interest was duly piqued.

Not long after she phoned the number on the card, she found herself on the books of the Brooks, Palmer & Stubbs Modelling Agency, which was based in a sprawling Victorian terraced house that lurked in the shadow of Archway Tower in Upper Holloway, and appeared to be painted completely white inside and out.

Charlotte had taken him there once, but he never ever went back. The toffee-nosed ponces who infested the building had looked down their noses at him as if he had just trodden freshly expunged horse shit from his Hush Puppies all over their Axminster. In contrast, Charlotte seemed to really like this strange alien world and rapidly took to the culture of chain-smoking skinny birds, agents with drawling toff accents and sleazy photographers who could frequently be caught fiddling with their underpants in between shots and wasted precious little time attempting to turn the aspiring young women into their own private harem.

Charlotte had begun to spend more and more time away from Chris and although he appeared to take it all coolly, deep inside it was burning him out. Their relationship had been blossoming, it felt like it had been growing almost day by day ever since their eventful trip to Southend the previous summer, but the new year had seen Charlotte move in another direction.

On paper nothing had changed but, in reality, Chris knew that everything had. Things were different and it hurt him. Now the only sign that she was part of his life was some make-up that gathered dust on the window ledge of his bijou bathroom and a few pairs of discarded knickers that lay in a pile under the bed. Maybe their big night out at the Barge would offer a rare moment of harmony. And a much-needed bunk-up.

'Gonna have fun in the city, be with my girl, she's so pretty…'

As Chris entered the pub, he could see through the crowd that Billy and Gaff were already there, sitting at a table with Evvy Boyle and Lorna Brady. The two gobby teenage girls had come down from Glasgow the previous summer with their friend Tracey MacAulay for the March Of The Mods gig at the Lyceum, on Wellington Street, and had never made it back to Jockland. Tracey had found the lure of the porridge and pipes to be too strong and had gone back home within a fortnight, but the two pals were gripped by the excitement and intensity of the young London Mod scene. So they crashed in a squat for a while until they got themselves jobs and a flat of their own.

The girls grew close to Chris and his mates but there were no romantic entanglements. Sexual entanglements were an entirely different matter of course. And at the end of many an evening if neither of them had got lucky, the girls often used the lads to 'fill in'. Both Gaff and Billy had enjoyed beer-fuelled amorous encounters with Evvy and Lorna on occasions and, although he was hopelessly devoted to Charlotte, Chris had partaken of a single bout of heavy petting with Lorna one night in a bus shelter on Poplar High Street. She later joked that if she hadn't had to get the last 15 bus home, she'd have taken him on a one-way trip to ecstasy.

The offer was probably still valid, but Chris hadn't yet felt the need to get his ticket punched. He scanned the room for any sign of Charlotte, but she hadn't arrived yet. It didn't really surprise him but it still made him feel that familiar sting of disappointment and anger. They used to be so close, so perfect… He sighed and walked over to where his mates were sitting.

'Where's Charlotte?' asked Gaff.

'Dunno. Don't care too much neither,' Chris replied, acting cool.

'Has love's young dream turned into a nightmare?' asked Billy, sounding a bit too happy about the prospect.

Chris sighed. 'Maybe. Maybe, I need some time on me Jack.'

'He's after Lorna,' laughed Gaff. 'He wants to adorn her, with large portions of horn-a.'

Even Chris laughed at that. 'Yeah well, me name is Christopher but I ain't no saint.'

Chris started to pull out a chair, but Billy had other ideas.

'Don't park your arse there, Davis, it's your round, son.'

Chris sighed again, theatrically this time, and made his way to the bar. The atmosphere at the Barge Aground was electric as usual and Chris soaked it up as he waited be served – smiles and style, laughs and lager, and the greatest music ever made.

Tonight, he was expecting a familiar mix of the Who, Secret Affair, The Jam, the Purple Hearts, Sam & Dave, the Small Faces, The Chords, Donnie Elbert, the Spencer Davis Group, the Teenbeats, Marvin Gaye, the Four Tops, the Ikettes, a bit of quality sixties Ska.

The soundtrack of the gods!

They had been coming here for less than eighteen months, and it couldn't have felt more like home if it had 'Chris Davis, West Ham, Mod, Palace of Crumpet' carved in giant letters across the front of the boozer. In the Barge, everyone seemed to know everybody else. Even walking through the door was like entering some great family get together. Not like a real family shindig with chicken in a basket and a bored DJ playing Olivia Neutron Bomb, Disco Duck and Peaches & fucking Herb either, but a gathering of like-minded souls who all shared the same love for the sounds and clothes and free-thinking, the precious essence of Mod – past and present. Timeless and perfect.

And the envious, middle-aged, middle-class rock press tossers, in their denim and dandruff-splattered tour jackets, would never ever get it.

Just thinking about Mod, what it meant and what it could still become, gave Chris a warm glow, even though the reality of it was that, just like families, in this scene a fight was never far away.

A big lump of a bloke, with a red potato-shaped face elbowed his way past Chris to the bar and shouted at the barmaid. 'Six pints of Carlsberg, darlin', as soon as you like.'

Chris gave the guy the once over. He was about two stone overweight. He was wearing an old suit jacket that was way too tight for him – so tight it would be a miracle if it ever did up again – a naff Motors T-shirt, drainpipe denims and Doc Martens. The typical uniform of the old punk looking for a new way forward.

Chris glanced around casually and spotted another five similarly dressed, newly arrived scruff-bags huddled around a table at the back of the club with two girls in black leather jackets.

'I'm next mate,' said Chris, keeping his voice flat and the tone neutral. Not angry or accusatory but measured enough to ensure that he at least got his first drink in before any fists started to fly.

'Well, you'll need to shout a bit louder next time, son,' the lump sneered. 'It ain't my fault the service in here is shit.'

He had bad skin and his teeth looked like tombstones on a fairground ghost ride.

Bev, the girl behind the jump, walked over to them, ignored Div Vicious and smiled straight at Davis.

'What can I get you, Chris darling?'

'Oh, is that how it is?' roared the lump, as he turned aggressively towards Chris. 'Go ahead, mate, I suppose it is your pub,' he spat sarcastically. 'Get your Campari and soda or crème de fucking menthe or whatever poof drink you lot go for and fuck right off.'

If his face got any redder, he'd look like a tomato thought Chris who felt an urgent need to deck the mouthy nuisance. Instead, he took a deep breath and ordered the round. It was too early for a ruck, even by his standards.

Yesterday's man leaned against the bar trying to give him what he imagined was a blood-curdling stare, but he clearly had nothing more to say.

Barmaid Bev gradually filled up Chris's tray with the drinks Chris had ordered. He casually sipped his Carling Black Label, and asked for a selection of bar snacks — crisps, pork scratching and Scampi Fries. He could feel the big lump attempting to glare some scares into him. Chris took another mouthful of lager before finally returning his stare.

'You're lucky you chose me to wind me up and I'm in a good mood,' he said evenly. 'If you'd tried that shit with any of my mates over there you'd be rolling about on the carpet by now.'

The guy pulled an expression of mock shock and yelped in a faux Charles Hawtrey voice. 'Oh, I'd better not mess with the Mod army, eh? You better check his ID, luv, he looks about twelve to me.'

Chris ignored him, as did paid Bev. He paid her for the round, gave her a wink that made her tingle and turned

16

to head back with the drinks. This was a bad development but a highly unusual one. This was a Mod boozer. The atmosphere when he'd first entered the bar was as warm and welcoming as it usually was. The Barge generally acted as something of an oasis on the mean streets of East London and its industrial overspill towns where everyone and his uncle 'wanted to know' and would cheerfully take a pop at any Mod they came across. Chris had been hoping for a night of laughs, lager, and a good leg-over – with or without Charlotte. If she didn't show, maybe he'd take a closer butcher's at that beautiful brunette sort he had noticed was now making regular appearances here. He certainly didn't want matey boy to put the mockers on that.

'I Can't Control Myself' by the Troggs had just started playing and Chris smiled. Glorious.

'Have a nice night,' sneered the lump. 'Enjoy your trip.'

The big fella thrust his leg in front of Chris's sending him crashing onto the carpet. The drinks went everywhere.

'You dirty fucking bastard,' roared Chris. He started up with the metal tray still in his hand but, before he could wrap it around the geezer's head, Billy appeared from nowhere and beat the bigger man to the ground with six rapid blows to the side of the face. Chris got to his feet and planted a kick of his own into the gobby irritant's gut.

Before he could land another, the lump's five mates swarmed into action, and both Chris and Billy disappeared under a flurry of boots and fists. The men were bigger, older, and this clearly wasn't their first rodeo. They weren't boxers or anything but they were hard and pretty keen.

Chris blocked the punches to his face, but their body blows were connecting. The odds were bad. Billy was still on his feet though and he knocked out one of their punky attackers with a light ale bottle.

Four against two. Better.

He was aware that Bev had started to scream and out of the corner of his eye he saw a good right-hander knock Billy clean off his feet. Now it was four against Chris, who had his back to the bar and no clear exit strategy. He kneed one in the nuts and kept his guard up, but he couldn't win this.

Suddenly time seemed to slow down. For every punch he was throwing, three were landing on him. He could taste his own blood and he was starting to see stars. But then he heard familiar voices above the barmaid's panic and the dull thuds of the heavy thumps he was taking. The cavalry had arrived. Gaff and a mob of other Mod regulars exploded like Vesuvius and were steaming into the older punks, punching and kicking them away from Chris and Billy. The Mods piled into the enemy with no mercy and no quarter. Never mind Wardour Street, this was an A-Bomb in Barking Broadway… it has blown up in the Barge, *'now it's spreading through the ciii'yyy!'*

Now it was the older punk gang whose claret was staining the carpet. Someone who had been watching too many Westerns, hurled a chair into the melee, bar-room brawl style, but it had little effect other than glancing off the knee of the semi-conscious berk who had started the ruck. Evvy and Lorna entered the fray too and stamped enthusiastically on enemy groins with their heavy black patent T-Bar shoes before spotting the men's leather-clad girlfriends cowering outside the ladies.

Seeing them coming in their direction, the punk girls retreated behind the toilet door but couldn't reach the cubicles in time. The Scottish Mod 'sorts' grabbed one apiece and delivered a couple of synchronised Glasgow kisses, so perfectly timed that they deserved their own film soundtrack.

Chris was still trying to shake off the dizzying effects of the beating he'd taken, but as he attempted to get back into the fight he stumbled and banged his leg on an upturned table. Billy proved far more resilient and he kept pounding away on the scruffy bastards before the pub landlord and his pal finally pulled him off. Despite the red mist, all of the Mods took Del's arrival as a clear sign to pull back. No one wanted to get banned from this little slice of Mod paradise, especially not the dealers among the firm; and besides Del had boxed for England and was mates with men whose names you didn't bandy about in public. Men who played by big boys' rules.

Only an idiot with a death wish would take him on.

The battered punks were lifted from the floor like so much garbage and bundled towards the exit. Their girlfriends followed them out sobbing. The few veiled threats that were thrown back at the Mods were drowned out as the DJ threw on the Speedball single 'No Survivors'. A nice touch. The Barge regulars cheered and drifted back to discuss the rumpus at depth over a gallon or two of cold lager, embroidering their accounts with every triumphant pint.

Gaff slung his arm around Chris and, pointing at the shattered remains of the drinks on and around his metal tray, said, 'Get a round in then, Davis, you tight bastard.' Both of them laughed.

'And don't worry about crisps, Chris, just get me a broken leg of lamb,' said Billy.

Chris grinned and tried to straighten out his crumpled clobber, dabbing at the worst of the blood and beer stains with a handkerchief. This was another whistle that would never see the light of day again. Laughing, Gaff gave him a light push in the direction of the bar. As he waited patiently to be served, Chris again felt an elbow brush against his. For fuck's sake, was this another thug punter ready to have a go? Would he actually get a drink tonight, because the night was starting to feel more like the undercard at York Hall.

He turned slowly, ready to growl at whoever was trying to give him ag, and was pleasantly surprise to see it was the brunette who had been catching his eye for the past few weeks.

'Oh, I'm really sorry,' she said. 'It's very busy isn't it?'

Chris just nodded as he caught his breath. She was even more stunning up close. She was perfect. Smartly dressed with perfect skin, and a sweet smell. Anais Anais? He wanted to nuzzle her neck.

To date, Chris had limited his observation of this wonder woman to furtive peeks across the boozer. He had liked what he had seen the first time she had entered the club, with a couple of other girls he didn't know, but as he was usually with Charlotte, he'd had to rely on furtive sideway glances to the times she went for a gypsy's. Now that the girl was by his side and in his vision, he was a little taken aback.

Her beautiful face was framed beneath a razor-sharp brown bob. Her large hazel eyes were like a warm blend of honey and caramel. Her slim body boasted a small but shapely bosom gripped firmly behind a black cashmere polo neck, and legs that were long and perfectly toned were barely clad in a tight black leather mini-skirt. Ding, dong!

Chris felt a warm, aching twinge in his balls, and beamed, before realising that he must have now been staring at her for several seconds like some saddo modernist sex case.

'Sorry,' he mumbled as he shook himself from his trance. 'I'm Chris, how are you doing?'

'I'm fine, Chris,' she said with a giggle. 'I'm Debbie. How are you?'

Her accent was East End, making her even more perfect.

'Fine, fine,' he rambled. 'Eh, can I get you a drink?' He turned slightly towards the barmaid. 'If I can ever get served.'

She smiled again. 'No, no, you're all right. I'm getting a round in for my friends.' She gestured over to the other two girls she was with, who were just as chic and almost as cute as she was.

'You go in front of me then, it's no problem.'

'No, you're okay. You look as if you need a drink more than I do…'

Chris looked puzzled. Debbie smiled and reached over to touch the front of his Ben Sherman shirt where a button had become detached. The back of her finger nails glanced across his bare chest shooting an electric bolt from the base of his spine to the back of his neck. Chris took a sharp, silent breath and then realised what she was talking about. His precious Ben had been ripped open in the ruck and his top two buttons were missing.

'You weren't involved in that barney, were you?' she said with a vague hint of distaste. Barney? He suppressed a smile at her archaic slang.

'The fisticuffs?' he asked straight-faced. 'Ah no, well, eh… my friends might have been…' His voice turned into a mumble and tailed off like a naughty schoolboy in front of the headmaster. 'It was them old punks that started it, I was just helping my mates out. Trying to put a stop to it.'

'There's always some idiot trying to start a fight, isn't there?' she said, pulling a face. 'I thought it would be different in a Mod pub, we're all her for the same thing, aren't we?'

21

'Yeah, they weren't Mods,' he said, not quite knowing how to answer her. Right now, he had one particular thing in mind but he was not sure it was the same thing that Debbie was referring to. He looked deep into her eyes and was away with the fairies again.

'I think you're getting served, Chris.'

He snapped back into focus, and saw barmaid Maureen, a bubbly mixed-race rude girl, waiting patiently. He ordered his round and cursed himself for drifting off again mid-conversation. He could only hope that Debbie didn't think he was some fucking glue-sniffing nutter or a thicko. But he couldn't help it. Debbie... Debbie what? Deborah Davis had a nice ring to it... as, he was sure, did she...

Debbie was something else. She was like some sexy Mod siren dragging him towards the rocks with her siren's call. Fuck Gloria, he thought, make it: '*D-E-B-or-ah, I'm gonna shout it all night long. Deborah! I'm gonna shout it every day. Deborah! Yeah, yeah, yeah, yeah, yeah, yeah...*'

'Thanks. Are you sure you don't want a drink?'

'No, but thanks anyway.'

She smiled warmly and he felt the electric bolt tingling once again. Chris put a ten pound note down on a beermat and then turned his attention to Debbie once again.

'So, do you come here often?' he asked. *Shit*, he thought, could he sound any cornier? 'Oof, sorry, that sounded like a creepy chat up line... I mean do you... do you... ah fuck it. I can't think of another way to say that that doesn't sound wank.'

Debbie laughed and gently patted his arm. 'It's okay, I know what you mean. Yes, I have been here before. I quite like it. My friends aren't so keen, and none of us like fights – they are so uncool! But the music is really great and there are a lot of cool people about.'

Maureen the barmaid tapped Chris on the shoulder and gave him a handful of shrapnel in change.

'Well, it's been nice to meet you,' he told Debbie. 'I'm sure I'll see you here again.'

'Yes Christopher,' she said with a coy smile. 'I'm sure you will.' She touched his arm and let her grip linger slightly too long.

Chris strode back towards his mates with a spring in his steps, a warm tingle sweeping across the back of his neck and a warmer semi growing in his Y-fronts.

Later that night, Chris and his mates stood outside the pub, smoking and nodding goodbye to some of the regulars that they knew well. Chris noticed a small tear on the knee of his trousers.

'Another pair of strides for the charity shop bin, mate,' said Billy.

Chris sighed. 'Never a dull moment in there, is there, Bill?'

'They should never have let the cunts in,' said Gaff with an edge of anger. 'Stevie fucking Wonder could have seen that they weren't Mods.'

'Yeah,' snorted Billy as he inspected his grazed knuckles and grinned. 'Maybe they need bouncers on the door.'

'Someone else for us to have a tear-up with,' laughed Chris.

'I don't think they'll be back in a hurry though,' said Gaff.

'Bunch of scruffy cunts,' grunted Billy. 'Were they from the poly? They looked like fuckin' students.'

'I'm pretty sure they were that mob from Becontree,' said Chris.

'You're not wrong, mate,' replied Gaff as he lit a fag and passed the packet round. 'That was their Barmy

Army for sure. They're balls-deep in old punks over there in hicksville. The bastards still think it's still 1977.'

'Thank fuck Dave weren't here,' added Billy. 'It would have been a fucking massacre.'

Gaff and Billy chuckled together and launched into a blow-by-blow account of how the fight had played out but Chris was getting bored and welcomed the sight of Evvy and Lorna coming out of the boozer.

'C'mon,' said Evvy. 'Let's find a chippy.' It was her and not Lorna who grabbed Chris by the hand playfully and tugged at his arm as they moved off up the Broadway. The others followed behind them with Lorna sighing theatrically as Billy and Gaff enthusiastically recounted their recollections of the scrap in forensic detail, some of it naturally embellished.

All around them were noisy mobs of pissed-up revellers who were staggering out the more ordinary pubs in the town.

'Do you think those dicks are still about?' said Lorna apprehensively.

'They'd better not be,' growled Evvy over her shoulder. The smaller-breasted of the two Mod birds was leading the way, striding along purposefully, still arm in arm with Chris as they turned into London Road. 'They've wasted enough of our fucking time tonight. If they try anything else I'll have their balls for earrings.'

'Oh yeah?' said Chris with a mischievous smile. 'You planning on putting your hands on some guy's tackle tonight then?'

'No, just yours,' Evvy cackled. She made a grab for his crotch. Chris fended off her groping hand and they play wrestled for a bit as they walked along, before finally stopping in a shop doorway to fall into a long, warm, sloppy kiss.

Something in the back of Chris's mind, maybe his conscience – God forbid! – told him that this wasn't the right thing to be doing. What if some grass reported back to Deborah? Or worse, Charlotte? But as he felt Evvy's firm body pushing against his with increasing urgency, his brains flew straight out of the window.

The skinny Scot seemed to be willing his hands to grab her arse and pull her forward against him so she could properly appreciate his budding hard-on. Eight pints of lager had inflamed his desire, and he had won the half-hearted internal argument by convincing himself that this whole encounter was Charlotte's fault, that she had forced him into it through the increasing lack of attention she paid to him. Where was she tonight? Why hadn't she called the pub to say she wasn't coming? Was she out boning some posh twat? His growing groundswell of self-righteous anger propelled him on and he knead Evvy's firm, boyish 'aris like fresh dough.

'Kneads' must when the devil drives…

'For fuck's sake,' interrupted Lorna as she strolled past them. 'Let's get a move on or the chippy will be fucking heaving.'

Chris had a proper lob on, though, and the pressure of it was making Evvy wetter than Lake Windermere. Both of them ignored Lorna and continued to kiss hard, their tongues poking and swirling about like conger eels with an escape plan. They kept snogging despite Lorna's tuts and despite the stream of low humour that Gaff and Billy directed their way. The pair had stopped right beside them and were both now gleefully taking the piss by making loud slurping and grunting noises.

Eventually Billy gave up, shouted out 'Get in there my son!' and walked off behind Lorna.

The pills, as yet undimmed by eight pints of beer, stoked feelings of guilt, alongside the brief images of

Charlotte that flashed inside Chris's head. But again he suppressed his weakness and kept going, allowing his hand to grab and caress Evvy's pert right breast. How could what he was doing be wrong when it felt so bloody good?

Evvy reached down and rubbed him, enjoying the hardness of his cock and the heaviness of the balls she now intended to drain. She drew away from his mouth, her eyes twinkling with mischief, and whispered softly in his ear, 'So are you planning a wee knee trembler tonight, Christopher, while your missus is out of the picture?'

'That depends on you,' Chris said urgently, cursing himself silently for replying so quickly – he didn't want her to know how desperate he was to get inside her. 'Will Lorna be back at the flat later?'

'Fuck that,' said Evvy with a frown. 'I'm no' waiting until then.'

She tugged his arm and started walking. 'C'mon, there's a wee alley up ahead just before we get to the station.'

He laughed. Proper Barbara Cartland stuff this, then…

Chris wondered momentarily how Evvy was so well acquainted with the town centre's al fresco shagging hotspots, but he gladly followed behind her admiring the way her firm buttocks swayed wildly inside her white leather mini-skirt as she walked ahead. Questions and doubts evaporated like droplets of specks of rain on a barbecue. The only thing running around his brain now was a Sham 69 song: *'I'm all right, I know what I want tonight, I'm gonna get my end away… I'm gonna get my evil way.'*

'Up here,' said Evvy urgently as she dragged him into a dimly lit alley. It reeked unpleasantly of overflowing bins, fresh piss and quite possibly a recently departed tramp or two. Not the most welcoming of settings, but Chris couldn't give a fuck. His throbbing boner was firmly in the pilot's seat now. For all he cared, they could have been in a padded cell in fucking Broadmoor as long as he got to split her whiskers, and plunge deep into that hot Scotch bonnet.

The light on the wall had long since busted but Evvy seemed to know her way. She dragged him into the darkness, towards a small doorway that was obviously the back entrance of some small shop, and kicked away the discarded remains of a fish and chip supper that lay on the step. Turning quickly, she fell back against the door and pulled Chris into a tight embrace. Their lips locked together and Evvy's tongue darted deep into Chris's mouth. His greedy hands slipped up the inside of her skirt and down the waistband of her flimsy pants in one fluid movement. She moaned gently and rubbed her thighs together rhythmically. As they kissed more frantically, Chris's fingers edged their way closer to the goal until they gradually found her warm moistness.

Evvy gasped and gripped Chris tightly around the neck as his fingers probed deeper. As the foreplay grew more frantic, she tugged wildly at his belt and undid the top button of his trousers, hell-bent on releasing his rock-hard cock from the constraints of his tightly contracted underwear and into the cold, fetid air of the back alley. Ah, yeah, come on, come out... and bingo – one nice, hard handful of Mod helmet, primed for action, as the song nearly said.

Right now, Evvy had the power. His desire was building up to desperation levels and she knew it by the way he was pawing at her cotton pants. But so was hers, and she didn't want him to come too quickly. With his cock in her right hand, she helped him tug down her drawers onto the grimy step below.

'C'mon, get me filled up,' she growled in her rough Glaswegian accent. Strewth, thought Chris, English birds aren't like this. At least not the ones he knew. But he was too fired up to care. He yanked up Evvy's mini-skirt and thrust towards her. She reached down and guided his heat-seeking Mod missile to paradise.

Chris bent his knees slightly to adjust his trajectory and when he knew that he had really made contact he began to pump firmly, a motion that set Evvy's bare arse tapping against the cold metal of the graffiti-blitzed shop back door. She lifted one leg off the ground to allow Chris's hard strokes to reach deeper inside her and then curled it around his calf for balance.

She was lost in her own world as her grunts and moans grew louder. Chris was thinking about football, trying not to peak to soon... until he heard something that froze him mid-stroke – it was a woman's voice and it was getting closer. Chris stopped thrusting and listened.

'What the fuck are ye doing?' grumbled Evvy. 'Don't say you're done already!'

'Shh,' he whispered. 'I think someone is coming.'

'Aye. Someone should be coming. Me! Don't stop for fuck's sake.'

Chris slowed to a steadier pace. The voices grew closer. A woman, no two women, but they were with some blokes and they had stopped at the top of the alley. Chris hushed Evvy again, and they paused completely, locked together and clinging on like limpets in the shadows.

'I think one of me fucking 'Ampsteads is loose,' moaned a male voice. 'Fucking Mods, they've bleedin' colonised that boozer. The bunch of lairy poofs.'

'We should go back there next week mob-handed and kick the shit out of them, get Big Bernie involved,' another angry male voice replied.

Chris twisted his head slightly and saw them at the end by the entrance of the alley. They were ten maybe twelve feet away. It was the Becontree punk gang from the Barge. He could see them pretty clearly now, although they couldn't see them. They looked plastered. They'd probably had a few too many in the Captain Cook, judging by the way they were swaying. He could probably do the lot of them on his tod, although he'd much rather finish rogering Evvy.

They started to move away when one of the rocker birds shouted "Ang on,' and came stumbling a little way into the alley for a piss, dropping her pants and squatting. The stream gushed out of her like urine from a horse, causing her to gasp with almost sexual pleasure.

It was then she noticed the couple in the shadows…

'Oi oi,' she squawked. ''Old on a mo, look at these two kinky bastards.'

The gang stopped and peered into the darkness. Their faces erupted in smiles. 'Get in there, chap!' shouted the big lump. 'Give 'er one of me!' shouted one of the others. The air was thick with laughter, abuse and no small measure of envy. Chris felt his stomach sink, this was the very definition of being in the wrong place at the wrong time. Separated from his mates, strides around his ankles and far from the protective eye of the few Old Bill who tramped the streets in pairs at weekends…

Luck was on their side though. None of the punks could see the coupling couple well enough to recognise them and when the punk girl had squeezed the last drop of moisture from her lettuce, they all moved on, back up towards Barking Station, muttering something about 'Rodeo and Juliet'.

Evvy laughed. Chris just heaved a deep sigh of relief. Only then did he realise that his Hampton was still standing firmly to attention inside Evvy's tartan tunnel of love. He kissed her softly on the lips and they both laughed out loud. He felt her vaginal muscles contract around him. 'Well come on then, Chrissy boy,' she badgered. 'Get it done for fuck's sake, I'm dying for a bag of chips.'

He reached his vinegar just in time for her to get to the chippie in order for her to be able to sprinkle hers on her rock salmon.

2

Saturday 19th April, 1980

For outsiders, Canning Town had always been
unwelcoming. Even now, as Chris trudged home in the
bleak emptiness of the pre-dawn hour, before daylight
cold spread an illusion of warmth over the deserted
streets, he was reflecting on the sense of unease a
stranger would experience here.

Probably rightly. Built around the old Royal Docks,
Canning Town and neighbouring Custom House were
now two of the poorest and most deprived parts in
Britain. Not just London, not just England. The whole
damn country. Voters might still return Labour MPs
here, but it's no cuddly commune. The docks had long
shut and these mean streets now belonged to hard men,
workers, boxers, armed robbers, hooligans, villains. You
watched your step and learnt respect.

Or you died. It was that simple.

Chris fished around for his key in the pockets of his
ruined suit. After his brief, backstreet bunk-up with
Evvy, they had gone on to a party back at the women's
place, where a slower second shag ensued, followed by a
four mile walk home in the cold, as the amphetamine
rush of Friday night slowly wore off, to be replaced with
the traditional comedown of Saturday morning paranoia.
He fumbled with the key in the lock and eventually
pushed open the door. The curtains had been left open
and the first shafts of early morning sunshine lit up the
pile of freshly-ironed shirts that were stacked neatly on
the sideboard beside his bed. Mum had been round then.

He could tell because the bin had been emptied as well, and a single plate and mug were gleaming on the wire rack next to the sink.

When Chris had first moved in, he was unsure if giving his mother a key was a good idea, in case she caught him mid-fuck on the bed at any time. But the old dear was fairly discreet and seemed to get the message – not quite 'if the room's a-rockin', don't come knockin',' more 'if the chain's on the door-y, I'm enjoying some amore…'

Chris's foot scuffed over a small envelope. His heart froze. He immediately recognised the handwriting on it and with mild feeling of dread he sat down on his dusty couch and ripped it open.

It was a 'Dear John' letter from Charlotte, a 'Dear Chris' letter to be precise. His eyes flicked over the lengthy handwritten text. It didn't really sink in at first but he understood the theme. It was the big kiss-off. Goodbye, thanks for everything, now sling your fucking hook. The tone of the letter was actually apologetic but at the end of the day the truth was stark – it was *sayonara* from someone who did not have the bottle to say it to his face. Someone he had loved.

Worse, someone he still loved. And someone he once thought he'd be loving for the rest of his life.

His feelings for Charlotte couldn't be turned off like a tap just because he had received some unwelcome mail, though. He'd known that things were a bit off between them for a while, he just hadn't expected their relationship to end like this. With a letter. So abrupt and so impersonal. He was also aware of the irony that his stomach burned with righteous indignation while his cock still reeked of Evvy's free-flowing fanny juices, but that didn't make the truth any easier to take.

He read through the letter again, trying to take it all in. All the clichés were there: 'It's not you, it's me', 'We've grown apart as people', 'Let's still be friends'. Blah, blah, fucking blah. What a load of bollocks. He was about to crumple the letter up and send it flying towards the bin when he noticed something else, buried in the text, something that leapt off the page and stung him straight between the eyes.

'Harold and I just fell in love, and it is something we just can't ignore, I hope you understand.'

Chris understood all right. Harold was Harold Halpin, the creepy toff photographer... the dirty bastard. He was the sleazy snapper who was always trying to get his models to reveal 'just a little bit more, love'. He was less half-in, more all-in every chance he could get.

Charlotte had slagged off the grubby old tosspot when she had first worked with him, describing him accurately to Chris as a 'a sleazeball' and 'a late 1960s throwback who refused to accept that he was in his forties'. Leather trousers, shirt open to the navel and always wearing some old band's satin bomber tour jacket.

Now it was love, eh?

Chris saw right through the no-good cunt from the off. 'Harold' was as transparent as the thin perm on the top of his head that passed for a barnet. Charlotte – *his Charlotte* – was destined to become just another notch on the old cunt's bedpost. She was smart, she was on the ball. How could she fall for that old pony? It didn't seem like the girl he knew, the girl that had been by his side through a blinding year of gigs, parties and long sleepless weekends.

Maybe he'd got her hooked on something. A little line of charlie after work? Or was it just the access he could provide to a brighter sparkling world of rich and famous parasites that had won her over?

Chris bowed his head as a sudden tidal wave of feelings swept through him. Every part of him ached from last night's bruises, his Hampton had started to itch and the brutal combination of hangover and speed comedown left him feeling like he should roll up in a ball and stay in bed for 48 hours. Total exhaustion threatened to envelop him. Chris forced himself up from the settee, crept over to the bed and flopped on to it without taking off any of his dirty beer-and-blood-stained clothes.

Fuck it! Everything seems better after a kip. Don't it?

***

Sometime later the killer combo of the pressure from his bladder and a horn-honking lorry driver conspired to rouse Chris from his fitful slumbers. He fumbled for his watch on the bedside table and tried to blink away the opaque sleep that cemented his eye lids – 4.47pm. Fucking hell, he hadn't really slept it was more of a black out. He'd been out for ten hours. Maybe more. Shit. Chris leapt out of bed swiftly. It was Saturday and there were things to be done. That was one of the parts of the Mod lifestyle that had burrowed its way deeply into his psyche. Sleep was an enemy to any budding modernist, especially at the weekends – an enemy to be overcome. 'I'll sleep when I'm dead,' was a saying he'd heard and a philosophy he adhered to. Leave kipping to the hippies and dole scroungers that were rotting in their fart sacks seven days a week.

In the modern world, it was always time for action... *Time to be seen!*

Chris's fingers fumbled over the switch for the kettle. He knew instinctively what he was about to do – shit, shave, bath (the flat didn't have a shower), then sling on his smartest schmutta and go out and find Charlotte Timms. Whether she wanted to be found or not.

He wasn't sure if he wanted to bollock her, beg her to reconsider or simply to tell the two-timing bitch to get the fuck out of his life. But whatever the outcome, it was something that had to be done face to face.

Chris caught a glimpse of some of her gear through the open door of his cramped bathroom. His first thought was to gather them up and chuck the lot of them in the bin. But he stopped himself, breathed deeply and decided to let them stay where they were. For now.

***

Chris always thought that Archway was an unusual location for Charlotte's model agency. The place was usual packed with drunken Paddies staggering out from smoke-filled boozers, malignant tooled-up soul boys and little mobs of Gooners... some ticking all three boxes. A fairly rum bunch. The offices of Brooks, Palmer and Stubbs were an oasis of middle-class propriety (and snobbery) in the neighbourhood, a place where ponces, toffs, models, and any puffed-up plonker who scraped their way to a diploma from the London College of Fashion could rough it among the 'common people' and ply their trade. It wasn't so much The Twilight Zone as a twat-heavy, toffee-nosed arty-farty one.

He pressed the buzzer next to the highly-glossed front door and awaited. Ten seconds later a haughty-voiced receptionist drawled something inaudible at him though a speaker. He grunted a monosyllabic reply and the door lock clicked off.

Chris strode up the barren but gleaming hallway, ready to meet the snooty gatekeeper. He found her almost hidden behind a huge marble counter. The woman peered over it with disdain from behind a pair of glasses so cartoonishly large that they would have given Dennis

Taylor a run for his money. Even though she was seated she still seemed to be looking down at him.

Chris snorted to himself in derision at the girl's bizarre clobber – an oddball blend of Weimar republic and Battlestar Galactica, a mix of old-fashioned lace, tweed, lurex and leather – but said nothing. There were legions of similarly dressed trendies lurking around Soho and there was a small freakshow parade every Tuesday night in Covent Garden as they made their weekly pilgrimage to the Blitz club in Great Queen Street – less than a goal kick away from that other beacon for the oddly dressed in the United Grand Lodge Of England.

'Can I help you?' she asked. Her tone was nasal and whiney, which made it sound as if each word she was saying took an extreme effort to expel from behind her blue lip-sticked cake-hole.

'I'm looking for Charlotte Timms, I believe she works here,' Chris said bluntly. The woman – girl really, up close, she looked barely nineteen – sighed and produced a large desk diary and removed a wad of A4 pages stapled together. The weekly roster? He could make out that it was a list of names, typed in alphabetical order, that she seemed to be actually checking through – despite the strain it was obviously causing her.

'Yeah, Charlie T,' she drawled. Even the nickname left a bad taste in Chris's mouth. She rang a number. 'Charlie? Uh huh. Uh huh. Thank you.'

She looked up at Chris. 'Looks like she is out on an assignment with Harold.'

'Do you know where?'

'No. I just know that she won't be back here today. Try again Monday.'

'Why thank you, sweetheart,' he said with a large side order of sarcasm. The sweetheart alone made her flinch.

Chris stood for a moment and pondered. An assignment? Hah. So that's what they were calling it these days. She was probably back at Harold's gaff getting a portion of wrinkly cock from the old sleaze bag. He scowled at the thought.

'Can I help you with anything else,' asked the receptionist in a tone that suggested helping him was the last thing on her mind.

Chris snapped out of his nightmare reverie. 'Why don't you try taking that stick out of your arse, and try and impersonate a human being,' was what he wanted to say. But what he actually said was, 'No, thank you. You've been most helpful,' because unlike most people these days he had manners.

He turned and marched stridently out of the building, imagining that he could hear the lazy posh bitch groaning at the gargantuan effort it took to press the button to unlock the door again.

***

Outside, Chris sucked in a lungful of fetid north London air as he tried to shake off the anger that was enveloping him. He found the only nearby phone box that didn't stink of piss and jammed a coin into the slot. No one was in at Billy's house. He wasted another 2p to find that there was no one in at Gaff's either. Slamming the phone down, he kicked open the door and looked for the nearest boozer. The anger inside him was rapidly turning to a unusual feeling of pain and longing. An alcohol anaesthetic seemed the perfect solution.

***

Street lights struggled to illuminate the darkest recesses of the Holloway Road as Chris tumbled from the Mother Red Cap boozer into the street three hours later. The strains of traditional Irish fiddly-fucking-dee music faded as the heavy door closed behind him. His shirt had the top two buttons undone and the once-sharp knot in his tie was loose and flapping. Chris steadied himself on a lamppost and smiled. Lager, Guinness and whatever else he had drunk had done the trick all right. Some of the old blokes in there really knew how to have a good time, even though bathing, shaving and dental hygiene were clearly off of their agenda.

The cold evening air stung him slightly and brought back memories of why he was spending Saturday night in the company of a gang of sozzled Paddies far from home. He immediately felt a mix of anger and resolve. Charlotte? 'Charlie T'! Fuck her and that dirty old cunt Halpin. She'd been holding him back anyway – sneering at his mates, wearing increasingly absurd clobber… and still banging on (and on) about Dave's violent antics at Southend. That was nearly a fucking year ago. Let it drop! Move on!

He was better off out of it. Maybe he could persuade Evvy to indulge in a bit of regular how's-your-father until he found a more local outlet for his ravenous libido.

Or better still, what about the lovely Debbie? Marc Bolan came into his brain unrequested – *'Der-der-der-Deborah, you look like a zeb-or-rah'* – and he smiled broadly.

'Watch where you're going, nonce!' A heavy shoulder prised Chris away from the lamppost and sent him spinning into the middle of the street.

'I wasn't going anywhere, you daft cunt,' spat Chris instantly as he struggled to get a firm footing on the pavement. As soon as he spoke, he realised the severity of his situation. There were five of them, mob-handed soul boys who were forming a circle around him. His eyes suddenly came into sharp focus as he identified the owner of the voice. Shit!

Richard 'Dick' Barton was only nineteen, but he already had a fearsome reputation. He headed up a very tasty firm of Gooner hooligans known as the Clock End Clan and had built up a small but lucrative business flogging weed and speed in the locality, as well as cocaine for a couple of the Arsenal team. His old man was the well-established underworld face, Dicky Barton, but the young Dick wasn't just another show-boating villain's offspring using their old man's reputation as a crutch. Dick would have been ruthless enough to succeed even if his Peter Pan had been Dick Emery's tea-sipping vicar.

The warm feeling that the alcohol had given Chris drained from his body like bath water down a plughole. Focus, focus, stay cool, he told himself, as his mind focused sharply on his predicament. It didn't look good. He was outnumbered, off his manner and in deep shit. And yet despite that he could not stop a wry smile drifting across his face as he took in with disbelief the soul boys' collective fashion sense. They were all clad in Lois jeans and sportswear apart from a hulking black bloke who was wearing denim dungarees over a bright yellow vest. Two of them even had those stupid fucking wedge haircuts that looked like they had a ripped curtain hanging over their ugly boats.

'What are you fucking smirking at?' snapped the smaller wedge wearer, the proud possessor of both a rat's face and comedy cross-eyes.

'Who does your barnet, the council?' replied Chris and immediately wished he'd kept his mouth shut.

'Cheeky cunt,' the small geezer exclaimed. He took a kick at Chris's groin that missed and hit his thigh. It was still hard enough to knock him off balance. Chris let out an involuntary gasp and tried to steady himself as he fell down onto one knee. At that point Barton stepped forward, put a hand under his chin and pulled him up until their eyes met.

'Nice whistle, bruv,' he growled ominously. 'You going to a funeral?'

'Yeah, his own,' cackled the small geezer.

'On yer feet, mate, come on,' said Barton calmly as he helped Chris up. 'No need for any unpleasantness.' Chris stood up, slowly and steadied himself, and Barton dusted down the shoulders of his suit lightly. 'There we go, Mod boy, looking sharp again. Now just empty out your pockets and you can be on your way.' Chris froze for a second as his mind turned cartwheels. He was desperately looked for an escape route but none were in sight.

Barton smiled. 'I know you want to make a break for it, pal, but you'd be wasting your time and mine and I've got too much to do.' He made a 'come on' gesture with his left hand. Chris knew there was an easy way and a hard way out of the situation, and either way he lost his dosh. But at the same time, he had been pissed about with way too much for one day.

He hesitated momentarily, and put his hand into his inside suit pocket as if he were fishing for his wallet. Then with a precision that belied his lack of sobriety, Chris barged forward, knocking the other, taller wedge wearer out of his way, and putting rat-face onto his arse with a backhander. But before he could get any further, the black guy grabbed him firmly by the shoulders and hurled him hard against the metal shutter of a shop doorway. CLANG!

Chris wheezed as most of the air was forcibly expelled from his lungs. As he gasped for breath Dick Barton gripped him by the throat and placed the tip of a Stanley knife close to his face.

'Now you really are wasting my time,' hissed Barton. 'That's why I'm glad I've got someone like Big Matt here to deal with any problems like this.' Barton smiled at the young black man and then turned his attention back to Chris. 'He's only a new addition to the firm but he's a useful geezer to have about. Now if you don't empty them fucking pockets, Matt is going to stomp you half to death and I'm going to stripe you so bad that your nearest and dearest will be picking up what's left of your face off the street when we're done with ya.'

Chris nodded glumly. He was beaten. No amount of heroics or backchat would do him a shred of good in this situation. He shrugged, sighed and pulled out his wallet followed by a handful of shrapnel from his pockets.

Barton eased his grip on Chris's throat, grabbed the wallet and back-handed the fistful of coins, sending them tinkling onto the road.

'There you go,' he hissed. 'No trouble. Just the way we like it.'

'What about his shoes?' piped up the angry, rodent-faced short-arse as he pointed at Chris's gleaming Oxblood tassel loafers.

'Too big for you, Stevie boy,' Barton laughed dryly.

'My brother can wear 'em when he's picking up the dog shit in our back garden,' protested Ratty.

'Fair enough,' said Barton. He turned to Chris again and said evenly, 'You heard him, scooter boy, get them off.'

'For fuck's sake,' protested Chris. 'You're not going to make me walk home in my fucking socks?'

Blam! Barton buried his fist deep into Chris's gut. As he fell, three of the others stepped up and took a kick at him.

'You're lucky you are walking home at all,' roared Barton, who turned his head away sharply and stopped talking. Chris followed his gaze and realised that the Clock End cock had been distracted by the sight of an older geezer leaving the Mother Red Cap, seeing what was going on and then quickly moving back inside.

Dick had crossed swords with Irish navvies – Cockney Reds to a man – before, but he preferred it to be on his own terms.

'Get his Scoobies and let's get fucking moving,' he commanded. The Gooner soul boys gave Chris a few more kicks and then retreated, moving off swiftly in the opposite direction to the pub.

'You had a choice,' yelled Barton in the distance. 'There's always a choice.'

Chris thought it was an unusual parting comment, but then he felt a wave of nausea at the back of his throat and he became far more concerned about not puking on his suit.

A small firm of Paddies poured out of the public bar clutching pool cues and bottles. They looked disappointed to see the soul boys beating their retreat. The first geezer shook his head in Chris's direction and shrugged as if to say, I tried. Then they reversed back into the Mother Red Cap leaving Chris to take a slow walk home in his socks.

This time as he arrived back into his flat, the first shafts of dawn were grudgingly seeped into the room, giving it a dull grey tone. There was no sign of any visit from his mother, let alone Charlotte – some hope! Nope, everything was exactly as he had left it.

Chris sighed. It had been a hard road back across London and his feet hurt like buggery. What a fucking day. He had lost his girlfriend, his wallet, his shoes, his self-respect and what felt like a tooth. He took off his grey tonic suit and tossed it into a corner of the room. He could probably write that off and all. The back was sticky from the nicotine-stained seats in the Irish boozer and the front was splattered with blood and some mystery stains from the pavement.

As he walked into the bathroom Chis winced. Various joints ached and the muscles around his stomach seemed to be on fire. He splashed cold water on his face then looked at his tired features in the mirror.

When you're young? He didn't feel young, not right at this moment anyway. From the corner of his eye, he noticed Charlotte's abandoned toiletries on the window ledge. Lotions, creams and perfumes all stood there silently mocking him. He swept his hand across the ledge and sent them crashing into the bath then staggered off to his bed, with the Purple Hearts' lyrics blaring around his head: '*I get frustration/I wear it like a suit/But the jacket fits too tightly and there's lead inside my suit...*'

3

Sunday 20th of April, 1980

For a Sunday night, the Barge Aground was surprisingly quiet. Chris, Billy and Gaff sat around a table near the door hoping to greet the familiar mobs of Mods as they turned up, but none of the regular faces materialised. Sure, there were a few nodding acquaintances scattered around the bar, but no major players and certainly no mates. And, as if to underline the dismal atmosphere, the DJ was a soppy stand-in with bumfluff and little more than The Merton Parkas and The Lambrettas in his collection to break up the succession of Northern soul standards. They weren't unpleasant, and they weren't the fucking Bee Gees, but they weren't the Purple Hearts either.

Chris pondered moodily at the sorry state of affairs. Surely this wasn't the beginning of the end? Okay, the 2-Tone thing was in rude (boy) health but they were all in the same boat, weren't they? It hovered a little too close to the cult of skinhead for him, but at least they looked the part in their sta prest strides and Fred Perry tees instead of ripped jeans, UK Subs t-shirts and the essence of glue around their chops. The Jam were still storming ahead and bands like Secret Affair, The Chords and the Purple Hearts were still releasing great records – even if they weren't all setting the charts alight. Fuck the mainstream music biz anyway, they turned out to be just as keen to bang a nail in Mod's coffin as they had been to profiteer from it less than twelve months ago. Only

Sounds and fanzines like *Maximum Speed* and *Direction, Reaction, Creation* afforded the music any respect these days.

The other downer was that a few of the older hardcore Glory Boys, disillusioned with Ian Page 'doing a Pursey', had drifted into following The Cockney Rejects who, on the plus side were claret and blue through and through. They were mates with Grant Fleming and Weller too, so they had to be all right, double all right in fact, but they were still a million miles from Mod.

Other than that, though, the scene on the streets had seemed healthy. Up till now at least. What kind of wanker would wake up and suddenly become a New Romantic? Ditching the timeless Mod look to mince about town looking like a camp Boris Karloff? And the blokes were just as bad. Fuck off!

Lost in his reverie, it took Chris a while to suss how irritated Gaff was getting. His mate was pissed off because his regular customers hadn't shown, and the hefty bag of black bombers was burning a hole in the inside pocket of his Harrington.

'You seen anyone, Mo?' Gaff asked Maureen the barmaid as she cleared away their empties.

'Evvy and Lorna popped in earlier, luv, but they didn't hang around. I think they were looking for you.'

'Ta,' grunted Gaff.

Billy watched her bend slightly to wipe down the next table.

'She's a sort,' he said, under his breath.

'I wouldn't mind,' said Gaff. 'Have you ever, with a black bird?'

'Not yet. But if Pauline Black came asking, I wouldn't say no.'

'What about Shirley Bassey?'

'Christ yeah. Hotter than a vindaloo mate, even at her age. Gotta be 40 something now.'

'What you, Chris?'

'Yeah, yeah. Put me down for a Body snatcher. What's her name, Rhoda?'

'Rhoda Dakar?'

'Yeah, she's a sort, and cheeky with it.'

Billy looked at Chris. Something weren't right. 'You're quiet tonight, mate. And you've only had one pint all night. Everything okay?'

Chris sighed. No it fucking wasn't. He had work tomorrow, he couldn't find Charlotte, and he still ached from the battering he took last night. Slowly and reluctantly, he told his two pals the full story of how he had lost his shoes, most of his cash and all of his dignity.

'Fucking liberty-taking cunts,' growled Gaff.

'We can't let that ride, mate,' said Billy.

'You know Dave's getting out this week, don't you?' added Gaff. 'This Wednesday.'

Chris immediately felt a stab of guilt. Dave had been nicked at Southend last August Bank Holiday, 1979. He'd kept in touch with him all through the court case and during his earliest weeks at Feltham. He had visited him regularly, too, but as winter closed in his visits became less frequent. He assumed that Gaff and Billy were visiting him as well. Both of them said they would. But early in the new year, he found out that neither of them had been near a visiting order since November. He knew that Dave would be pissed off, but instead of making amends, which would have been the smart thing to do, he simply put him to the back of his mind, mostly to concentrate on his crumbling relationship.

Yeah, he'd put a tart above a mate.

He wasn't proud of it but with so much going on in his own life, Dave had had to go on his 'Maybe Tomorrow' list and the truth is he had simply drifted from his thoughts. Out of sight, out of mind. He was chuffed that Dave was getting out, but knew that there would be some difficult conversations ahead.

'Where the fuck is everyone?' he said, with a hint of anger as he changed the subject while working off some anger by tearing a beer mat into a pile of shreds.

'They're probably over at that Russell Harty in Gidea Park,' said Billy casually.

'What fucking party?' Gaff exclaimed.

'That bird Terri Caesar that hangs about with the Hornchurch Mods, she's having a rave-up.'

'What the fuck are we doing here then, you dozy cunt?' spluttered Chris. 'No wonder there's no fucker about.'

Two geezers at the bar in Harringtons wearing Jam All Mod Con t-shirts turned and looked when they heard Chris raise his voice.

'No offence, gents,' Gaff said to them in a cheekily sarcastic tone that conveyed the message 'I couldn't give a rats' arse if you were offended.' The blokes looked pissed off, but returned to their pints.

Gaff looked straight at Billy and nodded his head. 'You daft cunt,' he said. 'I'm sat here like a spare prick at a wedding with a bag of bombers, a gram of sulph and a pocketful of blues. I could have shifted the lot at this little knees up.'

'But we always come here on a Sunday night,' protested Billy. 'I thought that's what you wanted to do?'

'Not when there's fuck all happening,' retorted Chris. 'Have you got the address?'

'Yeah, it's in here somewhere.' Billy began rummaging through the pockets of his parka. 'Stanley Road or something?'

Gaff quickly drained his pint and banged the glass onto the table with a flourish. 'Let's get a bleedin' move on then.'

Minutes later Chris, Billy and Gaff were cruising up Ilford High Street on their scooters, all three of them were tingling from the bit of Gaff's *surplus to requirements* whizz that they had greedily snorted in the Barge bogs, and fortified by chemical confidence they were ready for action, or excitement, or anything else fate chose to throw at them. Chris beamed as he felt the cool evening air rush past his face. Most folks – or should he say, sheep – settled for another mundane night in front of the mind-rotting telly before getting an early night before the grind of the forthcoming working week, but not him, Gaff and Billy. They were buzz kids! They were going places. Okay, it might just be a be a few cans in a cramped living room on the outskirts of Romford but there was always the possibility that it could be much, much more.

It certainly beat the cold reality of a lonely night in his flat on his tod drinking himself comatose. The 'normal' life was death row for any young modernist boy about town. If his mates could have seen his face, they would have noticed something that hadn't seen for hours – his smile.

But then suddenly the smile vanished. Chris jammed his foot down hard on the brake pedal and his Vespa skidded slightly as he pulled up at a bus stop. Gaff had to swerve to avoid running right up his arse. He was parked up and striding over to Chris before he even had his scooter on its stand.

'What are you braking like that for, you twat?' yelled Gaff. 'I could have been brown bread you daft cunt.'

But Chris wasn't listening. His mind was elsewhere, his eyes were locked in middle distance.

'What the fuck are they doing up here?' Chris said quietly as he stared back down the road.

'Who are you talking about?' seethed Gaff who was still visibly shaking after his screeching emergency stop.

Billy left his PX 125 close to the bus shelter and walked over, illuminated by the headlights of the few cars that were passing them. 'What's going on?'

'This ring-piece decided to check out his emergency stop skills for no fucking reason at all, that's what,' spat Gaff.

'Those are the geezers that done me in Archway last night,' said Chris, still staring at some figures moving away from them in the distance. 'I'm sure that's them. Well four of them at least. I can't see the big black fella.'

'Dick Barton and his boys?' asked Gaff. 'Bit far from home, ain't they? Are you sure mate? This is way off their manor.'

'I'm sure it's them,' said Chris. He shook his head and seemed to snap out of his trance. 'Fuckin' bastards! The next time we see them and we're mob-handed they are fucking getting properly done.'

'What do you mean next time?' grunted Billy angrily. 'Let's sort the cunts out now.'

'But there's four of them,' Chris protested and the words were out of his mouth before he realised how weak he sounded.

'Three, four, five... who gives a flying fuck,' said Billy. 'We'll drive back up the road and if it is them... wallop!'

Gaff stared at Chris, almost goading him. 'Reach into your toolbox, brother,' he giggled. 'Time for action.'

Dick Barton, Pete Rocca and Johnny Sullivan stomped along the pavement while their mate Little Steve Stennett aimed a shaky stream of piss into a shop doorway.

'Hold up for fuck's sake,' he yelped as he shook the last few drops from Littler Steve. But the gang kept going and Little Steve had to run to catch up with them. 'Why the fuck are we walking like a bunch of mugs,' he continued. 'We've got plenty cash to get a taxi.'

Dick stopped in his tracks immediately and spun round to face Steve. As he glowered down at his mate his eyebrows knitted together in the way that was familiar to the other. They knew the appearance of Barton's monobrow almost always led to someone getting a thick ear.

'Yeah, we've got readies,' he spat, prodding his forefinger into Steve's chest so hard that the smaller man staggered back against a shop window. 'And we've got it to pay for the whizz. That's how this fucking works, ain't it? We flog the gear, we pay for the next lot, we sell that… it's the basic rules of commerce you fucking twat. We don't just piss it up the wall on taxis, fags, brasses and jazz mags. We're building a business here.'

Little Steve rubbed his chest and grumbled, 'I'm sure your old fella wouldn't mind us spending a few bob on transport, Dick.'

Both Pete and Johnny exhaled audibly. They had a bloody good idea of what was coming next. Dick hated to be reminded that the only reason they were getting started at all was because of his old man's fearsome reputation. Dicky Barton Snr had been, what the Old Bill like to refer to as, 'active' in the London underworld since the late 1960s. Drugs were his main business but he had branched out widely over the years and no longer relied on selling bags of moody weed to dopy hippies outside the Roundhouse to make a living. Barton Snr was never shy of dishing out a spot of GBH where required, and, along with some fairly lively business skills, he had built an empire that stretched from the Caledonia Road to Dalston.

Unsurprisingly, between all the drug peddling, protection and malicious wounding, he had little time for family life and young Dick had seen very little of his fearsome father when growing up. When the old man was around, it was his little sister Evelyn who had always got most of Pa Barton's attention, but Dick still worshipped him. It was only recently that he had grown to resent his infamous father's overbearing shadow.

The desire to prove that he was far more than just Dicky Barton's kid gnawed inside him almost all of his waking hours. He certainly did not appreciate Little Stevie – or any other fucker – reminding him of his predicament. And he knew that there was only one way to make his fun-sized foot-soldier understand that bringing up his old man's name could be painful. He'd start off with a headbutt, he thought. But before he could act, a beer bottle sailed through the dark and hit Little Steve square on the forehead. Surprisingly it didn't shatter, but a deep gash opened up across Steve's skull and he dropped to the ground like a sack of spuds.

Dick spun round in time to see a guy on a scooter deliver a flying kick to Johnny's balls as he skidded past. Johnny crumpled to the pavement as two more scooter riders pulled up. They dismounted and moved towards Barton with tyre irons in their grip.

Chris grinned as he saw Steve slumped against a doorway. As much as he wanted to put the boot into the little shit, he knew that Dick Barton had to be put out of the way first. Barton looked confused. Bless. Chris swung his tyre iron at him, but the Arsenal soul boy instinctively lifted his arm and his elbow took the full force of blow.

Chris moved to his left and delivered a stamping kick to Barton's stomach which put him flat on his back. Billy and Gaff had already beaten Pete Rocca into a stupor, and Johnny was still wheezing on the ground cradling his crushed nuts so they turned their attentions to helping Chris pound Barton.

Chris punctuated every kick with the same question, 'Where's my money?'

Barton wheezed loudly but said nothing. They stopped pounding him and pulled him into a seated position against the wall. With the rest of the soul boys in no shape to retaliate, Gaff and Billy pinned down Barton's arms.

Chris squeezed the thug by the throat. 'You owe me for a new suit and a pair of loafers, you flash cunt,' he spat.

'Who the fuck are you?' hissed Barton as a few specks of blood dripped from the sides of his mouth.

'He's taxing that many blokes he don't even remember them,' shouted Gaff, shaking his head in disbelief before giving Barton a hard slap across the boat.

'Ah, I get it,' sneered Barton casually after he caught his breath. 'You're the little Mod with the paddy mates from last night. Walking home in his socks like a fucking tramp.'

There was no alarm in his eyes and no fright, which unsettled Chris. This was a bad man to make an enemy, but what could he do? Even though Barton was beaten and clearly defenceless there was no real sense of consternation about him. If anything, an air of inevitability hung over him. It was as if he accepted that the odd kicking was just part of his career path.

Gaff was less bothered. He just slapped Barton hard around the face again and reaching into his jacket pocket.

'Time to pay up you lairy cunt,' Gaff grunted. But then he gasped, as he pulled out a roll of bank notes as thick as a barmaid's wrist. 'Fucking hell, bingo! What a bundle!'

Now Barton looked worried. He was way more concerned with losing the lolly than he was about getting a richly deserved kicking. Barton gritted his teeth and he tried to push forward to get a grip on Gaff, but Chris and Billy held him down.

'Are you fucking mental?' he hissed. 'Give me that back. Do you know who I am?'

'I don't know mate. One of the Village People?' snorted Billy. 'He looks a bit like the cowboy, don't he?'

'We've got what we wanted,' said Gaff quietly, as he felt the weight of the wedge in his hand. 'Let's fuck off.'

'Just take what we need,' said Chris in a rare fit of diplomacy.

'Fuck that, he's got it coming,' laughed Gaff. He pocketed the readies in his parka and walked back to his scooter. Billy jumped up sharply and planted his boot firmly in Barton's balls.

'Come on, Chris. It's party time.'

'Right behind you.'

Chris took one last look at the wheezing thug and his battered mates as he walked away, and felt a deep sense of foreboding. It was the same kind of feeling he got whenever he thought of Dave's imminent release from prison.

It was a feeling that meant trouble was coming.

He paused but then shrugged almost invisibly. Maybe things weren't looking so bright, then again maybe it was just that moody sulph of Gaff's bringing him down. On the plus side, he could now afford to get his replacement whistle hand-made in Savile Row.

The nagging doubts evaporated pretty much as soon as they got to the party. The house itself was fairly nondescript. Typical semi-detached suburban drum. But inside the place was buzzing, and not to The Sound Of The Suburbs neither. Shona, the sort who was hosting the rave-up, welcomed them in warmly and accepted their gift of six cans of Skol and a bottle of Blue Nun without too much of a sneer. The place was packed full of faces from the usual Barge crowd along with a few others who Chris had spotted out and about at The Wellington and the Bridge House.

This was a proper sussed crowd, all packed in together, looking sharp. 'Baby Please Don't Go' by Georgie Fame and the Blue Flames was parping out of a creaky music centre in the background. While the rest of Hornchurch slept, the ravers kept going – their weekend went on forever. Happy days. All of the depressing thoughts and fears vanished. Chris rarely needed reminding of what being a Mod was all about but this gathering was confirmation indeed. He drank it all in, smiling like a dope, and as he scanned the room something else made his speed-fuelled heart skip a beat. Over in the corner of the room talking to two other girls was Debbie, the beautiful brunette from the Barge, the one he'd chatted to after that brawl with the Becontree punks, the one he'd thought of while he was pogering Evvy al fresco.

She was throwing her head back and laughing unselfconsciously at something her mate had said. He blinked to clear his eyes. The girl seemed to literally have a sparkle around her, an aura of personality and charisma. Uppers, minimal kip and the constant whiff of two-stroke fumes sometimes made his peepers burn, but Debbie's very essence was a soothing balm – along with her good looks of course. Moments before she would have noticed him staring at her like a stray dog outside a butcher's window, Chris snapped himself out of his trance and strolled forward confidently.

Nothing could fuck the night up now.

'Debbie?' he said softly.

'It's Chris, isn't it?' she said with a grin. She was asking but he suspected that she had remembered anyway.

'That's right,' he smiled. 'Good to see you again. We were over at the Barge earlier and if it'd been anything more like a fucking ghost town, I reckon Caspar would have dancing on the ceiling.'

He looked around the room, and added casually, 'I didn't know it was all happening over here.'

'Oh, yeah?' she said in a slightly mocking tone. 'I thought you were one of the faces.'

He took the dig and grinned, and then shook his head a bit. 'Been doing your homework, have you? Asking around about me?'

'Maybe,' she said coyly. She bit her smooth bottom lip lightly. he two other girls sighed and giggled at the blatant love ritual that was playing out before their eyes, and, after giving Debbie a quick knowing glance, they mumbled something and headed off into the kitchen.

Debbie patted the warm cushion of the couch that her friends' arses had just vacated, and Chris dropped down into it. She turned around to face him slightly and, as she repositioned her knee slightly further onto the seat, it exposed an extra few inches of her smooth inner thigh under that short skirt. Chris couldn't help himself. He eyed her legs greedily.

'My face is up here,' she said, chiding him playfully, and he turned a slightly deeper shade of pink. 'No need to get embarrassed,' Debbie giggled. 'It's perfectly normal.'

He liked the sauciness in her tone. Deborah knew what she was doing, although he wasn't sure she appreciated just how much of an effect she was having on his tenderest moving parts. All of his feelings about Charlotte seemed to have done a bunk; he felt so desperate to get closer to her that he took a gamble and moved in for a kiss slowly. The taste of warm lips or a slap across the dish were the only two outcomes – luckily Debbie was up for the former.

They kissed long and hard in a grinding embrace until Debbie pulled back slightly for a breather.

'You don't waste any time, do you?' she purred, as her hand dropped down to his thigh. A friendly pat, or an invitation to take things further?

'Knew I had my eye on you, did you?' she laughed. He didn't, but he gave a somewhat unconvincing shrug to suggest that he did.

'What are you doing tomorrow?' he asked as he wiped his lips gently with the back of his hand.

'Why? What have you got in mind?'

There was a huskiness in her voice that heightened his anticipation.

'Madness are kicking off their new tour down in Margate. It's at the Winter Gardens. I've got a couple of tickets. We could go down on the train… if you fancied it…'

'You've got tickets already? Were you planning on taking another bird before you met me?'

Chris momentarily lost the power of speech.

'Just Gaff or Billy,' he grunted. Then he noticed her smile and realised she was teasing him and added, 'But they can fuck right off.'

'Oh, yeah. Why's that, then?'

Chris pulled her a little closer to him and said evenly, 'Cos they ain't got what you've got.'

'Yeah? What might that be?' She sounded coquettish now as she pushed her firm breasts lightly against Chris's chest. Her perfume filled his nostrils and he felt an instant reaction below. He squeezed her body a little tighter and moved his face closer to hers.

'Come on, I'll show you,' he whispered. He moved in to kiss her and she didn't draw back. His desire, already rock solid, now threatened to overwhelm him. He tried to slip his hand just a few inches further under Debbie's hemline, but her hand clamped down on his and held it firmly. She pulled back from the kiss, just far enough that he could feel her warm breath on his face.

'I'm not getting touched up in public like some backstreet brass,' she hissed. She sounded fierce. Had he gone too far, moved too quickly? He opened his mouth to apologise but her tone softened, becoming more welcoming.

'Not here, Chris.'

Not here! So somewhere else, then! If his eyeballs were a slot machine they would have spun round and stopped on the jackpot signs.

4

Monday 21th of April, 1980

Chris stood outside St Pancras station and peered across the road at Kings Cross. It was late afternoon on a Monday, but things were already getting lively. Some old tom was arguing with one of her middle-aged 'clients' – all beer belly and balding hair – about God knows what. She slapped him hard, which presumably he might have enjoyed. Chris watched, enthralled by this living soap opera. The old brass walloped him around his swede with her handbag and her Elsie Tanner 'syrup' fell off. Two punks then grabbed the wig and started fucking about with it. Now the tom alternated between screaming foul oaths at them and hitting the old loser who she'd probably just sucked off in some back alley around the corner in Caledonia Street.

Chris giggled quietly to himself. There was never a dull moment around these parts. All human life was here! Two Old Bill turned up and got involved and now a small crowd of spectators had formed around them. The cops retrieved her wig and sent the punks on their way, but the tom carried on steaming into her John. So they nicked them both. Chris kept watching as they walked away, and noticed the bloke slip one of the filth a couple of notes. Hey presto, he was freed and the poor old prossie was the only one collared.

For some reason an old song his grandad used to sing sprung to mind: '*It's the same the 'ole world over, it's the poor what get the blame; it's the rich what get the pleasure, ain't it all a bleedin' shame.'*

He should have been at work of course, but the party at Gidea Park had lasted well into the daylight hours and even though he had just sat with Debbie all night it had been thoroughly enjoyable. They had alternated between kissing and chatting throughout and, yes, his probing fingers had been repelled on the few occasions that they tried to slide towards her gusset, he had not been disappointed.

He had a flashback of the moment they kissed as Frank Wilson hit the chorus on his Northern soul classic, *'Do I love you? Indeed, I do!'*

Love was a strong word, but Debbie was an amazing girl – bright, funny, feisty and unbelievably tasty, in both senses. He had always thought terms like 'love at first sight' and 'they hit it off immediately' were a load of horse shit, but in this case, with this bird, it was actually how it was.

In all those hours, he'd only thought about Charlotte once, but that thought was immediately relegated to the part of his brain marked 'who gives a fuck?'

When he'd left Debbie in the morning, she had promised to accompany him down to Margate. Chris had sat on the settee and promptly dozed off. When he came to, just before 10am, finding himself among various comatose teenage tickets in the living room, he rang his mum, pleading with her to phone his work and offer up some sickness-related excuse for his absence. After that it was back to his flat for the usual – shit, shower, shave and a shoe shine – before he ceremoniously pulled on his latest royal-blue whistle. He'd purchased it some time ago from Johnsons but it had yet to make its first public appearance. As he was getting ready, he stumbled upon Barton's neatly rolled up wedge which he had managed to eventually free from Gaff's grip with the promise that he would 'hold it' for their future endeavours. In the cold light of day, it looked like a heavy bundle. The thought that it had to be dodgy vaguely unsettled him but not enough to stop him from pulling out five scores and jamming them in his pocket before hiding the remaining bundle to the biscuit tin in the kitchen, placed above the cupboards and out of his mum's reach. He didn't want her to get suspicious and start asking questions, and he certainly didn't want her to find out how he'd come by it... He'd learnt long ago that you had to tread careful around mothers. Pretty much anything could set his old dear off.

Chris smiled.

'Have I missed something?' asked a woman. Debbie's voice was loud enough to snap Chris out of his reveries. Just seeing her made his smile broader than Hattie Jacques's aris. Debbie's brown bob was shining in the late afternoon sun, and her lightly made-up face was so smooth and beautiful he had to stop himself from stroking it. Chris cast a discreet eye over her firmly fitting white Fred Perry and casually looked down to check out her two-tone Jaeger mini-skirt, silky black tights and slip-on loafers.

'Well?' she continued, 'What's been occurring?'

Chris shrugged. 'You missed some old prossie kicking off,' he said. 'And a bit of bog standard police oppression. You know what it's like round here, Deb. It's like Casey's court, a proper fucking freakshow.'

He laughed briefly and she smiled.

'Do I get a kiss then?'

Did she get a kiss? She'd get more than that if only she'd let him. He lent forward, their lips locked together once again and, boom! that was it. The quick snog seemed to suck any tension out of their little bubble of atmosphere. Now they talked like a pair of long-time lovers rather than anxiety teenagers. They were so relaxed and chatty that anyone who saw them would have assumed they were a couple who had been together for years.

With a flourish, Chris pulled two tickets from his suit pocket and, after a quick look at his watch, they ran off into the station hand in hand.

***

Dick Barton and his mob strode along the streets of Hoxton aggressively. They were almost shoulder to shoulder, and moved like a platoon of off-duty squaddies; so much so that most passing punters assumed they were on a mission and gave them a wide berth. As The Last Resort sang, it was clear that they had violence on their minds.

Although the gang were all clad in almost new sports casual wear and mint condition trainers, their mugs told a different story. Dick, Pete, Johnny Sullivan and Little Steve all looked as if their faces had been danced by Big Daddy with a cob on. Only Black Matt, who had missed the previous night's messy tussle with Chris, Gaff and Billy, looked half decent. Barton felt no pain from his wounds though, not in comparison to the sting of shame he felt for losing the wedge, and the thirst for revenge that burned inside him.

'Are you sure about this?' said Pete in a slightly breathless tone as he tried to keep up with Dick's determined stride. 'Who the fuck are these geezers?'

'Look, they're all right,' hissed Barton as he continued pushing forward. 'We need gear. They've got it and they'll give us time to pay.'

'No doubt at a high rate of interest,' snorted Johnny. Dick stopped dead in his tracks and glared at his mate. 'Thank you, Geoffrey Howe,' he snapped. 'Have you got any better ideas, John?'

Johnny looked sheepish. He'd set Barton off on one. 'If you'd put up more of a fight last night instead of rolling around and clutching your bollocks we wouldn't need to be finding a new source.'

Barton turned his attention quickly to Matt, '... and if you'd been about, we probably wouldn't be in this mess.'

'I told you, I had a bit of business to sort out,' said Matt with a defiant shrug. He glared down at Barton, almost daring him to call it on.

'Business? You...' Barton was about to say 'you black bastard' but thought better of it. Instead, he went for a dry threat. 'You're the last one in this mob and if you keep going AWOL then you'll be the first fucking out.'

'Why don't we just get the gear from...' Little Steve was about to mention Barton's dad before he quickly remembered how painful bringing up that subject could be. '...eh, someone else,' he continued.

Barton shook his head. It was as if he was a teacher dealing with a classroom full of imbeciles.

'Look, we are getting it here,' he said firmly. 'Those fucking Mods have landed us right in the shit, but they'll get theirs soon enough. That's a cert, stand on me. Now there's the boozer over there. Let's get in, get what we need and get out. And for fuck's sake you lot keep quiet and let me do all the talking.'

The rest of the gang all nodded in either approval or resignation. Only Matt's face betrayed no emotion. Barton stretched himself up to his full height, 5ft 10, and led the way across to the Admiral Keppel. A big lump with a crombie overcoat and fawn slacks was on patrol at the door even though it was still early doors on Monday afternoon.

'What the fuck do you want?' he grunted at Barton's firm as they lined up in front of him.

He had big fuck-off hands – hands that could garotte a passing Yeti – and fingers like sausages.

'We're here to see Mr McVey,' piped up Dick with a swell of bravado.

'Not with that you ain't,' growled the doorman as he waved a dismissive finger towards Matt.

Anger flashed in Matt's eyes. Dick touched his arm to reassure him, and also to keep him calm. He'd wanted the big guy with him, but he wasn't going to push it.

'You hang here, Matt,' he said with an undercurrent that said keep cool, don't fuck things up. 'Keep an eye out for those fucking two-bob Mods.'

Matt glared at Barton, and then at the bouncer, but said nothing. 'Nothing personal mate,' said Barton as he made his way inside, 'Just business.'

Matt gave the bouncer a stare that would have chilled lava. He sneered back.

'Racist arsehole,' thought Matt. He turned and walked away silently and with dignity, and made his way down the street. He kept walking until he found a phone box, and then he made a call.

***

For Chris, the rest of Monday had sailed by like a dream come true. As they rattled along the rails to the coast he and Debbie had chatted, laughed and paused for the occasional bout of tonsil hockey.

The gig at the Winter Gardens had been blinding and, even though the venue was twenty times the size of the Dublin Castle, both the Nutty Boys and their support band – some hot Yanks called The Go-Go's – had kept the enthusiastic young crowd skanking and singing along throughout. Debbie was in her element and dancing around so eagerly that Chris had to choose several times between watching the bands on stage and ogling her bouncing Bristols.

The crowd were pretty cool. Okay, there were a couple of boneheads trying to stoke up some bovver and doing the sad old 'seagull' salute like the morons they were, but like most of the audience, Chris and Debbie were too preoccupied to take much notice. As the encores ended, they seemed to float out of the venue on a sea of euphoria that even the chill of the coastal Kent night air couldn't dampen. Hand in had, they headed for the beach front and found a bench over by the Clock Tower. He brushed off a handful of cold chips that were scattered across it.

'You're really into all of this, ain't you?' said Debbie, with almost a mocking tone to his voice.

'All what?' replied Chris, trying not to display an ounce of indignation.

'The Mod thing. All the smart gear... being clean and tidy, looking good. Some of the places you go are dripping with blood, beer and God knows what else. You'd be better off with a pair of jeans and a biker's leather jacket than a tonic suit.'

Chris shook his head in disbelief. 'That'll be the fucking day, all that scruffy clobber, dirty boots, no deodorant and bad breath... that will never be me.'

'So you've signed up for "clean living under difficult circumstances", then? Is that what it's all about?'

'You're quoting Peter Meaden, the real Modfather,' said Chris, who recognised the quote from a copy of Maximum Speed. 'Yeah, that's about right – our thing is about out-doing the middle-class scruff-bags, bosses, teachers, Old Bill, fucking social workers and the rest.'

She nodded and he carried on. 'But you know that and you're winding me up. You must be because you're not too far off being a Mod yourself with all the quality gear you wear.'

'I wear what I want, okay? I like The Jam and Madness, Secret Affair and that, but I'm an individual. I like other bands as well. I like wearing monkey boots but that don't make me a rude girl or a skin bird. All this tribalism, Chris, it's a load of bollocks. It's working-class kids beating up other working-class kids. Why? Because of the clothes they're wearing? That's mad, Chris. Boneheads rucking with punks? Teds and rockabillies fighting over the size of their turn-ups? What a lot of old pony! The only people winning are the elite, who look down their noses at the likes of us.'

Chris thought for a moment. He didn't agree entirely but he wasn't in the mood to argue and blow his prospects of a leg-over. Maybe she had some kind of point. He'd come back to it. Maybe.

Debbie picked up on his silence and didn't push it.

'My uncle was an original Mod,' she offered by way of breaking the deadlock. Chris nodded and waited for her to carry on. 'Him and his brother were the kings of Soho in the sixties.' Debbie could see that Chris's interest was aroused. 'He was always sharp, my mum said. He had made to measure Savile Row suits coming out of his arse... He don't look like that now though... more like Jason King.'

'I bet he's still smart though,' said Chris. 'That's what it's all about, you never lose it.'

'So, you're going to be cutting about in all this get-up years from now are you?'

Chris didn't even need to think about it. 'Course I am. This is not just a passing fad you know. Things might evolve but this is me.'

Debbie suddenly burst into the chorus of Shirley Bassey's 'This Is My Life' and her voice was tuneful but loud and clear enough to attract the attention of the few evening strollers nearby. Chris grabbed her in a playful cuddle and hushed her singing. 'For fuck's sake, you're full of surprises.'

'Yes I am,' she said with a grin and kissed him firmly on the lips. Then she lowered her voice and added, 'So why don't we take a little walk down on the beach and I can show you some more?'

Chris and Debbie walked along the promenade giggling at the drunken desperados staggering back to dismal cut-price B&Bs and the few square couples walking arm in arm as they took in the dying embers of the day. They moved down onto the sand and just kept on walking and talking until the crowds faded and the darkness swallowed them up. Sitting down on a deserted patch of sand close to the sea they huddled together for a moment simply for warmth but body heat, proximity and passion rapidly led to something else.

As their kissing grew more intense, Chris slid his hand up Debbie's inner thigh once again. He moved slowly but determinedly expecting her to clamp it still at any moment, but unlike yesterday evening, this time he met no resistance. He pressed his palm against her knickers and held it there. Debbie didn't push him away. His fingers touched the nylon gently at its middle point. It felt warm and damp in equal measure. She lay down on the sand and lifted herself up just enough for Chris to slide her tights and her silken panties down far enough to gain unhindered access to her welcoming box of delights. His index finger crept inside her. Deborah moaned lightly and he established a smooth, gentle rhythm. Her moans got louder and Chris applied himself steadily, suddenly realising that he was rubbing his fully-covered boner against the side of her thigh like a dog on heat. God, he couldn't wait.

But he had too. Debbie reached her final destination much faster than he'd expected. As her body erupted in a firework display of orgasmic delight, she gripped his shoulders so firmly that small flashes of pain shot down his back.

They lay there quietly together for a while. He waited patiently as she got her breath back and came floating back down to earth. Chris didn't have to wait long. Moments later he felt Debbie's hand brushing over his flies, feeling his hardness through the straining fabric. Oh yes! She fumbled with his belt in an increasingly frantic attempt to release the plump pink prisoner within. '*Any day now, any way now, I shall be released*,' thought Chris with a smile. Was that the Doors? He couldn't remember. It didn't matter because he could feel the cool night air circulating around him. Finally little Chris was free, and he was standing proudly to attention, ready for action in whatever form it came.

Debbie ran her hand over his cock. It felt like she wanted to caress every throbbing inch of him. Then, still holding him firmly, she kissed his cheek and slid herself down his body, teasingly slowly, towards it.

Chris drifted off into his thoughts. Getting a blow job on the beach would undoubtedly be a sexual fantasy for many, he thought. Just imagine if in Dr No, Ursula Undressed had gone that little bit further on the sun-kissed beach of Ocho Rios and given James Bond's 007-incher a proper noshing off... He grinned at the thought of Sean Connery yelling 'Yesh, yesh' as Andress got to work on his John Mac-Thomas. The image made him laugh silently but he quickly forced the daft thoughts out of his head. This was a special moment and he didn't want to miss any of it. Even if it was here on Margate beach after midnight, a romantic setting if you could just forget that the surrounding area was littered with stones, empty cans and Zoom lolly wrappers.

He could feel the sand, which was rough and damp, under his aris. He already knew that this suit would never see another night out, it was already as crumpled as a tramp's pants. But fuck it, he could always buy another whistle. The evening had had its fair share of compensations already and they were getting better by the minute.

Chris shivered a little as Debbie's warm, soft lips tantalised his little soldier. He had a feeling she had done this before. It was already the best blowjob he'd ever had as she alternated between playfully licking his helmet and then sucking away on him like a kid with her first lollypop – why did they call it a blow job? he wondered momentarily. There is no blowing involved whatsoever. Her cold fingertips tickled his balls and he tried to focus on other things – the privacy, the distance from the promenade, the incoming tide, West Ham's next home game – anything, to delay the inevitable.

Suddenly Debbie stopped what she was doing and stood up. Chris could just about make out her struggling to pull down her tights and pants in the darkness. Her top half was still clothed. Then she laid down alongside him. In preparation for a spot of missionary, he rolled onto his side but Debbie pushed him back firmly.

'You stay where you are,' she ordered. Yes boss.

She straddled him and lowered herself slowly onto him, guiding his shaft towards her warm moistness. She slid all the way down, accommodating his entire, not insubstantial length in one swift movement.

Welcome to the house of fun…

Debbie gasped. She was wetter than she had ever been. His cock didn't feel like some alien intrusion, but more like it was part of her. She pulled off, being careful not to release her dancing partner, and then she started to bounce rhythmically in perfect union.

Below her, Chris had banished all thoughts of the coldness and the damp from his mind as he savoured every moment. She was in charge and he didn't mind that. Chris could feel an eruption building in his balls. He wanted to come but managed not to – it was hard to feel desire and not surrender to it, but he planned to let her finish and then reverse their positions, and Chris could feel from the changes in the breathing that she wasn't far off. As soon as Debbie started to gasp loudly, he held her softly, let her climax and then held her closer. She dismounted and laid on her back.

'Your turn,' she said.

He didn't need telling twice. Chris was up on his knees and between her legs. She guided him inside her and his plans for a little finesse went out the window. Instead he just hammered away like a carpenter on piece rate.

It was all over far too quickly. Chris reached a shuddering climax and collapsed onto her for a moment before rolling off and laying back on the sand. He stared up at the stars and smiled contentedly. Why couldn't every Monday night end like this?

Debbie rolled closer and they kissed softly. Maybe it hadn't ended yet…

5

Tuesday 22nd of April, 1980

Several hours and two bunk-ups later, the cold reality of their beach bunk-up had become all too apparent. The mojo-driven modernists were cold, uncomfortable and their clothes were damp and probably beyond repair. Those famous golden sands didn't look quite so tempting now. The sober realisation that Chris hadn't once used a condom hit them both at around the same time, but remained unsaid.

'Fancy a walk?' asked Chris.

'I thought you'd never ask.'

They stood up, and pulled their dampened clobber back on, and then they wandered along the promenade for a while before the early morning drizzle that seems to plague most English seaside towns became so unpleasant that they ended up huddled together in a dilapidated bus shelter for warmth. It meant they could watch the sun rise over the North Sea. It looked vast as it burst through the mauve clouds into a sky the colour of a grapefruit, yellow with hints of orange. But the cold combined with the sticky mess of their underwear took a lot of the allure out of the heavenly spectacle.

'I don't know what I was thinking leaving a bed and breakfast out of my trip down here,' mumbled Chris.

'If I'd known we were staying, I'd have brought a change of clothes.'

Debbie didn't sound angry, just a little embarrassed. He didn't know what to say. Chris had, of course, always aspired to get his leg over something more than a scooter last night, and now he was mentally kicking himself for not planning ahead (as well as hoping for head).

Rather than speak, he lit a fag in the vain hope of creating the illusion of warmth.

'Why didn't you bring your scooter?'

She sounded sleepy, but sexy. The thought of knocking up a landlady and spending the morning in a double bed having double bubble and double egg on endless toast flashed through his mind, but he knew she had to get back. Maybe she'd be up for it if he cheered her up.

'I wanted to have a drink at the gig, Debs. And besides that, there are so many thieving pikey bastards down here it would have probably ended up in the back of some battered Transit van while we were watching the band.'

He held his hand out. The drizzle had stopped.

'Shall we, madam?'

'Oh yes, Sir Christopher.'

They wandered up the prom leisurely. Their train home was still hours away. Maybe the cafés would open soon. An early morning mist was sweeping in slowly off the sea, reducing the early morning dog walkers and joggers to mere smudges in the distance. They strolled past the entrance to Dreamland to kill some time but it did not look all that dreamy with the big wheel immobile and the rollercoaster shut. The paintwork needed touching up and without the candyfloss and laughing suntanned kids, the funfair was just a silent chunk of art deco brick and glass looming over the road and intimidating the row of tat-filled shops all around it that promised fish and chips, ice cream and novelty crap but still had closed signs in their door. Even the arcades were shut.

Debbie seemed to be thinking the same thoughts. 'Don't these fools realise there's a market for early morning kiss-me-quick hats?' she asked with a giggle.

'I could do with an early morning start-me-up coffee,' he laughed.

'Just coffee? I'm disappointed.'

'Don't tempt me.'

'Maybe they do teas at the station?'

'Good call. We ain't got long to wait.'

They reached Margate station. Chris took a quick peek at her. She still looked hot enough to melt a 99 – despite the lack of sleep and the wetness of her clothes. He had probably seen more of Debbie since they first got together at that party in Gidea Park than he usually saw of Charlotte in a week. Since her modelling work began, she had barely been around, flitting in and out of the flat at unusual times and always boring him to tears with tales of anorexic models, high society gossip and posh-boy photographers – usually when she rolled in pissed on Moet after a work event. Or non-event with nonces, as he saw it.

By the end, he'd been lucky to get a bunk-up once a fucking fortnight. Maybe if he'd smeared his old chap with Beluga caviar it would have moistened her gusset and made a difference...

Margate station was like stepping back in time. It had a cavernous booking hall that was as cold as a Siberian mortuary. Almost as soon as they walked in, Chris noticed two skinheads lurking in the background, giving it the big 'un, laughing loudly and filling the ears of the few early morning passengers who were trying to get to work with foul oaths and leery chat. They of course immediately noticed Chris and Debbie.

Chris pulled her back.

'Be careful here. Skinhead alert. Stay casual and look to your left, four o'clock.'

He watched the two skins huddle together and murmur to each other like conspirators in a bad stage play. Chris breathed deeply through his nose. This was going to kick off, he could feel it.

'Fucking boneheads,' Debbie spat quietly.

'Our train is in. Let's hope they're not on it.'

They walked about two thirds of the way down the train and found a carriage that was relatively empty. No one was following them. Chris felt flushed with relief. He sat opposite – a better view he felt than the window seat. Deborah produced a glass perfume bottle out of her clutch bag and sprayed herself and her clothes. He couldn't make out the label, but the smell was unmistakably her.

'Did you have a good time, Deb?'

'The best,' she said. He noticed she was blushing. He leaned forward.

'Then we'll have to do it again. Better planned next time.'

She nodded and smiled. Happy again.

It was then that Chris spotted the brothers bonehead swaggering up the carriage behind her – where had they come from? They must have ducked in the first carriage and walked up inside the train.

'Sit next to the window, babe.'

'Why?'

'Just do it.'

Chris tensed up and prepared for the inevitable. As usual the smaller of the two would-be hard cases piped up first. He was a weasel-faced moron with a tear tattooed under his left eye and 'cut here' across his throat. It was a tempting offer.

'Which one of them do you think is the bloke, Knocker?' weasel boy guffawed.

Knocker, the larger man, laughed mindlessly at this sparkling wit but said nothing – maybe his muscles had colonised his brains, thought Chris. He was a big bloke but not much bigger than a walk-in wardrobe. Obviously not much smarter either.

Chris gave them the once over. The scruffy bastards couldn't be further removed from real skinhead style if they were wearing kaftans and flowers in their barnets. Skinhead had come from Mod. It was a working-class alternative to the hippy end of Mod's youth cult evolution. Skinhead music, like original Mod music, was also black – Ska, soul, reggae. These soppy cunts were wearing British Movement badges.

He sighed. Chris knew right away that this was going to be more than a war of words and the inevitability of that angered him far more than usual. He was tired, cold and simply wanted to spend the rest of the journey cuddled up next to Debbie. There was never any peace being a Mod these days. Just one ruck after another. It was like he was living in the English equivalent of The Warriors. Every gang who crossed his path, every subculture, every little street mob wanted to know.

Dave would love this, he thought, but it wasn't what he'd got into the scene for. Looking good *was* the answer, but it seemed to piss off every other bugger in a major way.

'Keep moving, you mugs,' Chris hissed, in the full knowledge that there was zero chance of the two apes taking his advice.

'You'll be moving to Margate General, you fucking ponce,' growled weasel boy. In almost perfect synchronisation, he and birdbrain both produced two sharp, gleaming Stanley knives.

Weasel boy moved closer. That was his first mistake. Instinctively, Chris kicked out from his seated position and caught him squarely on the knee. The bonehead grunted in pain and fell forward. The tip of the blade dug deep into the fabric of the chair a few inches from Chris's ear. Leaning backwards, Chris managed to get both of his feet against the weasel boy's chest and propel him backwards, straight against Knocker. The larger skinhead's blade, which was still in his outstretched hand, dug deep in weasel boy's back.

As his mate screamed in agony and fell to the floor, Knocker dropped his knife and tried to clamber over him to get at Chris, losing his balance in the process. Chris was out of his seat like greased lightening, punching Knocker in the face and the side of his head as rapidly as he could. The big lump was still trying to get over his mate who was groaning on the floor. He lost his balance and gripped onto the chairs at either side of him as Chris continued the pummelling. The train started to shake a little as it slowed down for Herne Bay. Chris grabbed Debbie's perfume bottle and smashed it over Knocker's head. He could hear her screaming but that did the trick. Knocker was out like Elton John.

Chris took his opportunity, and dragged the big lump a few feet to the train door, leaning him against it. He did the same to weasel boy, dragging him down to the next one, allowing his head to bounce off the handrail to keep him KO'd. Then he rushed back, collected both Stanley knives – just in case – and mopped up the broken glass with a discarded Daily Mirror.

At Herne Bay, unlucky passengers joining the train were shocked when they opened the doors to be greeted by a plummeting bonehead, both falling like circus tumblers but with far less grace. 'Drunken hooligan,' said the little old lady who had just missed being hit by the comatose weasel boy. That made Chris laugh a lot. He was worried that his display of ultraviolence might have put Debbie off him, but if anything it had the opposite effect. With other passengers on board, a bit of how's-yer-father was out of the question, but he soon felt his girlfriend's toes gently stroking his groin.

He looked at her, and she returned his gaze and shrugged 'What?'

'Nothing,' he replied. 'Everything is hunky dory.'

Debbie was sipping a cup of tea and Chris was absent-mindedly stroking his bruised knuckles as the train pulled into Faversham fifteen minutes later. Normal bods and commuters crowded the platform but, in the background, he heard the not-too-distant sound of male voices chanting. As they grew nearer, the words became clearer: 'Sham Army! Sham Army! Sham Army!'

Chris looked at Debbie in disbelief. 'What the fuck is going on today? It's only Tuesday morning and yet the lunatics are out in force.'

'Just ignore them, Chris,' said Debbie as she gripped his arm a little. 'The arseholes are everywhere. Even you can't take them all on. Nobody could.'

Chris nodded silently in agreement but he suspected that once again his resolve was about to be stretched to breaking point. After almost a quarter of an hour of peace, three punk yobbos burst loudly into their carriage. Chris and Debbie were the only one of the passengers not hunched behind newspapers in a desperate attempt to appear invisible, so naturally they stood out like a Russian tank in Coronation Street.

'Oi, oi,' yelled the first punk. 'Time for action.'

The other two chuckled loudly. All three of them were Billy Idol rejects. Short, spiky blonde barnets, scruffy bikers' jackets and ripped, bleached denims struggling to avoid the top of their heavy DM boots.

'Nice tits,' blurted the leering yob closest to Chris and Debbie.

'Which one?' snorted another, who was wearing a Sham 69 lapel badge, over a smaller metallic Millwall one.

Chris's 'fight or flight' mechanism was firmly switched one way after his recent rumble with Weasel and Knocker, but despite Debbie's whispered instruction to 'let it go', the three berks had now made any form of appeasement unthinkable. Leaping to his feet, Chris lashed out at the nearest punk and delivered a well-filled knuckle sandwich that left the gobby moron groaning on the floor. He moved into the aisle and swung at the 'nice tits' joker, but his fist sailed past his ear and the punk grabbed him in a headlock and started dragging him up the carriage as his pal aimed punches up and down Chris's back and side.

'Leave him alone, you bastards!' yelled Debbie. She tried to leave her seat, but the punk Chris had put on his back scrambled up from the dirty floor, grabbed her arm and pulled her back into her seat.

'Just sit down, darling,' he snarled. 'We'll deal with you in a minute.' He grabbed her left breast, caressing it roughly. Debbie was meant to be intimidated but his coarse assault had the opposite effect. She shot back up, grabbed her metal tea pot with her right hand and smacked him around the side of his head as hard as he could. The force sent him flying. As he tumbled, the punk hit his forehead against the arm rest of a chair and he landed on his back. Debbie screamed gutturally and delivered a firm kick to her target's crotch, but the geezer was spark out. The burning pain of aching bollocks would have to remain a little treat waiting for him when he regained consciousness.

She noticed a bag of glue had fallen out of his jacket pocket. In seconds she had emptied the lot of it over his face.

'Sniff that,' she muttered.

Along the corridor, the other two punks stopped beating up Chris and gawped at their mate out cold on the floor with cheap adhesive rolling slowly into his nostrils.

Done by a bird! The indignity!

'What the fuck have you done you crazy bitch?' gasped the one wearing the Millwall badge. They ran down to their fallen comrade. The first one was almost crying. He fell on the comatose nuisance and started cleaning his face with a grotty piece of tissue, muttering 'Bruv, bruv' repeatedly.

Chris shook his eyes back into focus. His ears were ringing but he realised that the train was slowing down and that the third punk was now squaring up to Debbie.

Chris ran down behind, knocking him flying.

'Deb, Deb, come on, quick.' He grabbed her as he ran over the knocked-out mug, casually using his stomach as a walkway, and reached the door just as the train pulled in to Gillingham station. They opened it and jumped out while it was still moving, fully expecting at least one of the punks to be on their tail, but nobody came.

As they walked up past their carriage, they could see their shocked assailants. Well two of them. Gluey was still on the floor, they one Chris shoved out of the way was nursing a bloody nose, and Millwall was just staring at them, his mouth hanging open in disbelief.

The whistle blew and the train trundled off down the track.

Chris looked at Debbie and they both laughed.

'What the hell was that?' he asked, genuinely surprised by the turn of events.

She smiled and kissed her knuckles comically.

'Didn't I tell you my dad had boxed for England?'

Chris smiled. 'His blood matched your nails; how did you manage that?'

'Voodoo.'

They laughed, embraced tightly and dived into a prolonged bout of tongue-wrestling that drew despairing glances from a couple of old dears who were wandering past clutching shopping bags.

Thirty minutes killing time in Gillingham would normally feel like an eternity, but Chris and Debbie found the now deserted waiting room for some more heavy petting and the half hour just flew by. They jumped on the next train, Chris concealing his arousal under a discarded copy of what she called 'Her Majesty's Daily Telegraph'. They found a free table and settled back for what he hoped would be a sedate fifty-minute journey back to the Smoke watching the Kent countryside roll past.

Chris was knackered. They both were. He thought about having a quick kip, but decided against it. Life was too short to sleep!

'Don't nobody work no more?' he asked with a chuckle. 'Seems to me there are just loads of geezers travelling around on British Rail looking for a ruck. That's what awaydays are for!'

'It's Fatcher's Britain, ain't it luv,' said Debbie in a heavily exaggerated cockney tone loaded with mocking sarcasm. 'Loads of deprived dole scroungers with nothing to do but spend their waking hours prowling the mean corridors of shit trains hunting for mods to beat up.'

They both laughed.

'Well it's something to tell our kids about,' he said, fake-seriously.

'Oi!'

'You remember jokes don'tcha?'

'Only the funny ones.'

They were still in a jovial mood as the train approached Bromley South station.

'Here we go gorgeous, round 37,' said Chris with a smirk. 'Who's going to get on here? Angry Teddy Boys? Pissed-up Rastas? Ultraviolent hippies? A mob of soul boys?'

The laugh froze in his throat as he peered out of the window. There were a group of six or seven 'herberts' – football hooligans – on the platform, their mix of green combat jackets, straight leg jeans and trainers made them stand out distinctly from the older travellers in the station who all appeared to be dressed in various drab shades of brown or grey.

'I don't fucking believe it? Is today Youth Cult War Day or something?'

'Get down,' snapped Debbie. They both dropped down onto the sticky floor under the table out of sight. They could hear the lads walking past their window and they held their breath until the voices subsided. As the train moved off, they stayed down there, stock still, waiting for the sound of boisterous teens in Adidas trainers marching towards them, but it never came. For the next five minutes they remained in their cramped hideaway, pissing themselves with laughter.

'Tell me a joke,' said Debbie when they emerged. 'I want to keep laughing.'

Chris thought for a moment and said, 'A punk is shagging his girlfriend in the toilets at the Marquee with loud music blaring out. The bird says, "Is this Johnny Rotten?" he says, "Nah I've only used it twice."'

'Filth,' she replied in a way that didn't make it sound she was bothered.

'You do one.'

'Okay. A virgin boy is about to have sex for the first time with a more experienced woman. He's had a strict Catholic upbringing and asks her "How will I know if it's indecent?" She says, "Don't worry – if it's hard enough and long enough, it'll be in decent."'

Chris was in stitches. They were still laughing when the train rolled into Waterloo – mercifully free of street gangs – and making their way across London on the tube.

Debbie asked if he was worried about anything, and for some reason Chris just opened up about the Dave situation. Debbie thought about it for a moment and told him straight, 'If he's your mate, and you care about your friendship, you've got to be man enough to apologise, face to face.'

Chris nodded. She was right.

***

When they eventually reached Chris's flat, the thought occurred to him that he might just have left it looking like the SAS had just raided. He fumbled with his keys in the lock, pondering what kind of excuse he could cook up to excuse it. But fuck it. It is what it was. She'd have to take him as she finds him one day. Why not now? He swung the door of his flat open and graciously made a big show of letting Debbie in first.

'Oh, such a gentleman.'

'Of course! Would you expect anything less?'

Debbie smiled, took off her coat and hung it on a peg. Chris looked around. It was half-tidy. His mum must have been round.

'Jesus!' he said, as he closed the door behind him. 'Home at last. What a journey. Is there anyone under twenty-five using public transport these days who isn't after a fight?'

Debbie laughed. 'Cruising for a bruising is what my Scottish gran would call it. But I worked it out, Chris. Pretty obvious when you think about it. They weren't all pissed off because you're a Mod – they were all pissed off when they saw that you were with me. It must have driven them all into a jealous rage.'

He loved it when she joked like this. It made her eyes sparkle more than normal.

Debbie walked around the small flat seemingly giving it the once over.

'Oh yeah?' he replied sarcastically. 'You reckon you can turn geezers who get a butcher's at you into raving lunatics, do you? That they see what they want and can't have it and it drives 'em nuts?'

'Maybe…'

She ran a finger coyly across the dusty window ledge.

'Oh sorry, the maid must have missed that,' he joked. 'I'll have the butler horse-whip her on the morrow!' Chris paused. 'You don't seem too bothered by all of that aggro. Is that normal life to you then?'

Debbie made a little parping sound with her lips. 'Boys will be boys,' she said. 'It's not the worst thing I've seen. One morning when I was, I don't know, six or seven, I came down for my breakfast and found my uncles, the Mod ones, with some strange bloke. Uncle Steve was holding him, and Uncle Kenny had a rolling pin in his hand. The stranger's trousers were down around his ankles and his nuts were on the kitchen table exactly where I was planning to sit and eat my breakfast. They had tied a tea towel around his mouth, to muffle his noise, and Uncle Kenny started whacking his cobblers with the rolling pin. My dad saw me, got me a bowl of Rice Krispies and just took me into the living room to watch *Mary, Mungo and Midge* as if it was perfectly normal to see something like that in your own gaff. For them, maybe it was.'

Chris raised his eyebrows and winced quietly.

'What kind of what were your uncles into?'

'Accountancy,' she said deadpan. And then both of them laughed.

'Can I use your loo, Chris?'

'It's there.'

Debbie relieved herself and then checked out the bathroom cabinet, which still contained Charlotte's perfumes, nail varnish and a lipstick. 'They'll have to go,' she muttered.

She washed her hands and walked into the living room, which was a bit of a dump. Debbie noticed some of Charlotte's clothes stacked on a chair by the windowsill and shook her head. Was he hanging on to her memory or just too lazy to chuck it down the shoot? She spotted his long players lined up neatly next to his Radiomorelli record player. Secret Affair's 'Glory Boys' was at the front, with The Jam's 'All Mod Cons' behind it. Next were Mods 'Mayday 79' and 'Quadrophenia'.

He came in from the kitchen and said, 'The Chords' album comes out next month. Can't wait! I've got the kettle on, fancy a cup of Rosie?'

'Very domesticated. Yes please. Two sugars.'

She followed him back into the basic looking kitchen.

'It's okay,' he said. 'Not a rolling pin in sight.'

Chris had started to feel a bit ropy. The after effects of all that scrapping on the train had started to announce itself in the form of throbs and aches all over his body. After today, even the bruises would have bruises.

He reached up for a couple of mugs and winced.

'Are you all right, Chris?' asked Debbie.

She had a note of genuine concern in her voice which pleased him.

'Yeah, just a few side effects of the day's adventures.' He filled up the tea pot and carried a tray loaded with milk and a bowl of sugar through to the living room. Debbie picked up the digestives and joined him. She flopped down onto the worn settee. Chris spotted a small tornado of dust rise up into the ray of sunshine that was peeking through the curtains and blushed. He needed to get this place spic and span.

He eased himself down beside Debbie and another involuntary grunt escaped from his lips.

'Oh, my big handsome boy,' she said in caring, matronly voice. She smiled briefly and then she jabbed four fingers sharply into his ribs. Chris exhaled and bent forward quickly clutching his side. Debbie laughed like a drain.

'You're supposed to dodge the punches, babe. You'll need to stay ready if you're in the business of defending my honour from all the troglodytes out there in the mean streets of East London.'

What the fuck? What have I got here, Chris wondered, a refugee from the fucking Kray family? Still, it was rare to find a bird who looked like a dream, and who could handle herself and who had a cracking sense of humour. There was no way he was kicking her into touch over a bit of heavy-handed horseplay. She was a tough cookie for sure but a fucking gorgeous one.

Debbie stopped laughing and reached over and unbuttoned two of the buttons on his Ben Sherman before slipping her left a hand through his shirt and letting her fingers wander.

'Let Nurse Deborah give you a little check-up,' she purred. 'Show me where it hurts.'

Chris undid the whole shirt and pulled it open, revealing a patchwork pattern of purple marks.

'For fuck's sake. You don't do anything by halves.'

She paused for a moment with an extremely wicked glint in her eye. 'Maybe a little lip service will sort you out.'

Debbie leaned forward and placed her soft lips on Chris's solar plexus region so lightly that it was almost ticklish. She continued to plant small kisses all over his front and as the pain in his body subsided the throbbing down below became increasingly apparent.

'What's happening here?' she said coyly. 'It looks like you might have some dangerous hardening of the arteries going on here, young man.'

'It's another injury, nurse. The throbbing is something awful.'

'I feel that I had better examine the area,' she said with a straight face as she undid the flies of his royal-blue strides. With a quick fiddle she managed to unleash the beast. Little Chris now stood proudly to attention – clearly craving more attention.

'Hmm. There appears to be some stiffening going on here,' she said, staying in character. 'It could be early onset rigor mortis. Does it hurt when I do this?'

She pulled his foreskin down to reveal his helmet and then pulled it back up.'

'Yes, nurse.'

'And this?' She reached down and massaged his testicles.

'Oh yes. I think there's some bruising there too.'

'Yeah? Well, I better have a look, then.'

He raised his backside off the settee so that she could pull down his trousers and pants. Then she cradled his nuts in one hand and softly massaged them again.

'Hmm,' she said, finally, pulling a face. 'I can't see any bruising, young man... Nah, it looks all right to me. I think you're telling porkies, son.'

She sat back alongside him, affecting disinterest.

'I think the bruises are invisible to the naked eye.'

Debbie laughed then moved a little closer to his lap. 'You fucking chancer... okay I had better give you a CT scan then.'

Chris hoped against hope that the CT wasn't short for Cock Tease.

It wasn't. Deborah gently slid her lips over the top of what his wank mags would call 'his straining helmet' and then sunk down, taking almost his entire length into her mouth in one swift action. Chris let out an involuntary sigh of pleasure and sank deeper into the couch as her tongue worked its wonders. As cures for a battering go, this one worked far better than a couple of aspirin and some physio...

Just before he closed his eyes, Chris noticed that Charlotte had left behind a Kate Bush LP that was propped up against the wall on the other side of his record player from his own collection.

Shit, if Debbie had seen that... That's going straight in the bin, he thought with a giggle before he groaned contentedly and drifted off into ecstasy.

6

St George's Day. Wednesday 23rd of April, 1980

Chris shivered as he stood outside the gates of Wormwood Scrubs. It was not particularly cold but just being near the notorious 'shovel' gave him the creeps. He was convinced that he could actually smell the stench of sweat, slop-out buckets and despair.

It occurred to him that if it carried on the aggro-ridden life he was living, with one bloody scrap following another, could easily lead to a spell of bird for him too. All it took was for someone to get seriously hurt or a wrong'un to grass him up… he had to cool it.

The sound of metal hinges creaking open chased the thought away. Some lucky jailbird was about to walk free, for a few months at least.

The first bloke out had been in so long that his suit was almost back in fashion. The geezer pulled up the collar of his bum-freezer jacket and looked around fruitlessly for the loving welcome that never arrived. The man shook his head and snorted in dismay, and then started to walk down the road to the nearest bus stop. A couple more pallid old lags shuffled out and took a deep breath of freedom before they were greeted by small groups of family and friends who were loitering around the gates.

Dave was the last one out. Chris had to look twice to make sure it was him. He looked a mess. His five o'clock shadow looked closer to midnight, and his hair was like a patch of overgrown garden weeds. Walk around Carnaby Street like that and even the tramps would turn their noses up. Hiding his surprise, Chris walked towards him with his hand outstretched.

'Excuse me, mate, I know you're on the way to a Hawkwind gig, but have you seen my mate Dave?' he joked. 'Bloke about your height? Sharp dresser? Well-trimmed barnet?'

'Very funny,' grunted Dave who pointedly ignored Chris's proffered hand. 'Very droll. I've just spent nine months clenching my arse cheeks together in the shower and all I get on me way out is a comedy routine.' His tone changed from tired to aggrieved with a side order of sarcasm. 'Who are you anyway? I've spent so long in there without any visitors that I can't fucking remember.'

Chris stared at his feet like a naughty child for a moment then tried to offer some kind of explanation.

'It's just… well, I eh… ah, fuck it. I feel bad, Dave, really bad, but if it counts as any kind of excuse I've had a lot on me plate.'

Dave didn't look impressed.

'I broke up with Charlotte.'

Dave stopped glaring at him long enough to suppress a yawn.

'And there's been no end of aggro – soul boys, boneheads, punks. All of 'em tooled up.'

Dave was a little more interested at the thought of rucks and rumbles, but he wasn't going to show it yet. It'd wait.

'I take it Billy and Gaff have no excuses either,' he said with an edge of anger. 'I never saw either of them lazy fuckers either.'

The two friends just stood there, like a portrait of awkward silence, for a moment that seemed to last minutes. Then the jail doors slammed shut with a clang behind Dave. He gave a shiver then started to walk away.

'C'mon, let's get away from this fucking place.'

'Yeah.'

Chris handed Dave a spare crash helmet. 'I'll take you for some nosh mate. My treat. There's a caff up the road that does a lovely bowl of warm porridge.'

'Very funny,' said Dave quietly with a tiny hint of a smirk on his lips. 'Very funny indeed.'

In the café, Dave was eating like a geezer on death row. First one all-day breakfast, then another.

Chris was smiling on the outside while worrying exactly how much his treat was going to set him back… until he remembered that he had grabbed Barton's cash on the way out just in case his mother was poking her beak about in the kitchen while he was out. He patted it nervously, just to make sure it was there.

He checked out his old pal's scruffy demeanour once again and tried to progress the necessary conversation with a degree of diplomacy.

'Bet you can't wait to get a shave and a decent haircut, eh?'

Dave shrugged his shoulders and then leaned forward conspiratorially as a few drops of egg yolk escaped from the side of his mouth. He spoke quietly, as if he was still worried a screw or a prison grass might overhear him.

'Never mind that,' he said. 'What's been going on? In reverse order of importance, why did you give Charlotte the fiddler's elbow, who are the mugs you've been having tear-ups with, and why the fuck have you got a roll of bank notes that would choke Red Rum in your sky rocket?'

'Oh, you noticed that did you?' Good old Dave. He hadn't changed then. Villainy was always top of his agenda.

'Yes I fucking did.' Dave leaned even closer. 'So, what's the deal with the wedge? Is there more of that? What you got going?'

Chris sat back in his seat. The closer Dave got the stronger the smell of chokey became.

'It's nothing. It was a one-off thing. Some mob jumped me and we were just taking back what I was due. It's over.'

Dave laughed and more breakfast morsels hit the Formica tabletop.

'You don't take that much money from someone and it's *over*. It don't work like that bruv, and you fucking know it.'

Chris pushed the plate with his half-eaten bacon roll to the side of the table. The day had started shit and it didn't look as if it was going to get any better. He had thrown another sicky at work to pick Dave up. but he knew he would not get paid for it. Now here he was in a greasy spoon listening to his jailbird mate work out involved plans for revenge on people he did not even know.

A week that had started with a bunk-up on the beach and a blow job the next day, was going downhill faster than Buster Bloodvessel in a well-greased barrow.

Slowly he spilled the entire Who-sized can of beans, about Dick Barton and his soul boys, the punks in the Barge, the fights on the trains – the first thing that made Dave laugh – and finally, with a little careful editing, a tall story about why he'd elbowed Charlotte and replaced her with Debbie. After all, chances were Dave would never ever see Charlotte again. It's not like there was any Venn diagram where their social circles intertwined.

By the time he'd finished, Dave seemed a lot cheerier. 'I've got one question, has Debbie got a sister?'

Chris laughed and told him about Evvy and Lorna.

'Any port in a storm,' grinned Dave. 'And talking of ports, any chance I could flop at yours until I sort meself out, mate? It'll only be for a few nights.'

Chris groaned internally. He didn't need a flatmate in any form, but how could he turn Dave down?

'No problem. You'll have to kip on the settee.'

'I'd sleep in the bath to be honest, Chris. Anywhere would be better than that fuckin' flowery.'

***

Forty minutes later they pulled up to the flats on Chris's scooter, only to find that there was another visitor waiting on the doorstep at the entrance to the block. It was Charlotte. What the fuck? Her eyes were red with tears and she looked as if she had spent the night kipping in a skip. As she got to her feet, Chris instinctively wanted to comfort her in his arms but he checked himself and stopped a few feet away from her. Charlotte sensed his reluctance to get too near and she started to sob uncontrollably as she flopped down again onto the step.

While Chris struggled to make sense of what was going on, Dave took the initiative.

'What's up, Charlie love?'

'Dave?' said Charlotte through a veil of salty tears. 'Is that you?'

'Don't you fucking start an' all.' Dave pushed his hair down as if to make himself more recognisable, and, thought Chris, less like Worzel Gummidge's lovechild.

Chris stepped forward and helped his ex to her feet.

'What's going on, C?' he asked, trying to sound aloof but not inhuman. 'C'mon, love, let's go inside and put the kettle on. The nose-bags round here will be loving this. Better than fucking Crossroads.'

Once inside the flat, Chris sat Charlotte down on the couch – in the same place nurse Debbie had seen to his throbbing pain just before. He went into the kitchen to make a brew, while Dave wandered around taking in his temporary home. It was as if he was a little unsettled to be in a room without bars and one that more importantly did not smell of piss and sweat. Eventually he flopped down in the armchair as if he was claiming his throne.

Chris returned balancing three mugs of builder's strength tea, and handing one to both of them, before perching next to Charlotte, still trying not to get too close.

'So what's all this about?' he asked.

'It's, it's that bastard Halpin,' she said, forcing back tears. 'He's thrown me out, Chris. He said things weren't working and I had to go.' She paused for another sob before carrying on. 'I'm sure he's got another girl somewhere but that's it. We're over, just like that. No remorse.'

'Classic pump and dump by the sounds of it,' parped up Dave in the background. 'In it and bin it, fuck it and chuck it.'

Charlotte howled even louder.

'Dave, for fuck's sake, you're not helping, mate,' Chris hissed. But then he struggled to find any words of comfort for his weeping ex. Part of him, the rotten, malicious selfish part, felt that he should just laugh triumphantly and show her the door but the residual of love he felt for her and some nagging feeling of sympathy stopped him.

'Maybe it's for the best,' he mumbled almost inaudibly. 'The bloke was a cast-iron cunt. I told you that when I first saw him…' He kicked himself for playing the 'I told you so' card. 'Maybe things are…' he paused as if he was scouring his brain for words of wisdom but there was nothing forthcoming. 'Fuck it, I don't know what to say,' he sighed and shrugged his shoulders.

Thoughts of Debbie flickered through his mind and looking at Charlotte in her distressed state he wondered if he had not done too badly out of their break up. 'What is it you want, Charlie, I mean why come here? I thought you'd washed your hands of me. And of us.'

Charlotte wailed even louder.

Maybe she thought she was going to be welcomed back with open arms, he thought. That maybe she'd open her legs and all memory of her betrayal would fly out the window. And maybe now she has realised that was not the case.

Charlotte struggled to compose herself and when she felt calmer. 'It's just my jewellery, my purse and some cash my parents had given me for my birthday,' she sniffled. 'He's kept the lot. Took my key, told me not to come back. He threw some of my clothes into a suitcase and left them outside the studio but that was it.'

Dave flipped forward quickly as if the slop-out bell had just rung.

'That no-good thieving cunt. That's bang out of order,' he snapped. 'That cowson needs sorting out.'

'What's it got to do with you?' snapped Chris.

'Somebody does your bird over and you do nothing? What kind of bloke are you? Have a word with yourself,' spat Dave.

'She's not my bird. We'd split up. Days ago.'

'Days ago?'

'A week maybe.'

'Piss off,' sneered Dave. 'I'm not interested in who did what and why and where and all that old bollocks. All I know is that someone who was one of us, someone who you loved, has been turned over by some snide old cunt and you, you want to ignore it cos' – he adopted a camp accent – "We'd split up". That's double bollocks, Chris.

Where does this piece of shit live, Charlotte? Gives us his address and we'll get your tom back.'

'Oh, we will, will we?' muttered Chris under his breath, but a painful sting of embarrassment had hit him right where it hurt – his conscience. Dave looked at Chris with a mix of disdain but he said nothing. For the first time today, despite the haircut, he looked like Dave. His eyes positively twinkled with the prospect of carrying out some righteous retribution for a damsel in distress.

Charlotte gave him a warm smile. She ripped an advert out of the copy of Sounds that was on the table, picked up a pen and scribbled down an address.

'This is where he lives.'

'Toad Hall,' laughed Dave. He snatched the paper greedily from her hands and the keys to Chris's scooter from the side and started to walk out.

'What? We're going now?' asked Chris, but Dave was already out of the flat and heading for the stairs.

'Time to get the old team back together,' he shouted, the words echoing ominously in the concrete stairwell. Chris followed him half-heartedly, but he was already revving up the PX.

***

Chris looked at his ex-girlfriend on his settee. The tracks of her tears could not disguise how beautiful Charlotte was. Part of his brain was calculating how hard it would be to talk her back into bed, but the smarter part of it realised he had to get her out of his drum quickly, just in case Debbie turned up unannounced.

Tough. But not impossible. He put his arm around her for a sympathy cuddle and said, 'Listen, I can't let Dave do this on his own, just in case Halpin's not on his Jack. Write that address down for me, please Charlotte. It could go tits up for both of us, so you had better not stay here. Can you go to your mum's – just for now? I know you'll be safe there.'

She cuddled him back and sobbed again. 'I, I thought you'd hate me,' she stuttered. 'I wouldn't blame you if you did.'

'I could never hate you,' said Chris, with all the fake sincerity he could muster. 'Never.'

Charlotte kissed him on the lips. He responded and the peck became a full-on snog.

He pulled away. 'Give me the address and let me get after him. We'll have time to talk about what happened, if you want to.'

She scribbled the address down on a Debbie Harry advert – sacrilege!

'I do want to, I want to apologise.'

Chris smiled inwardly. 'Let us get your gear back. Then we'll have all the time on the world.'

He walked her down to the bus stop and she kissed him again. He'd be slipping her the goldfish in no time.

***

Knowing Gaff and Billy would be at work, Dave went straight to the barbers to smarten himself up and then drove on to the Durham Arms. He struck lucky. Both of them were there, drinking after-work lagers and playing the fruit machine.

'Did your VOs get lost in the post then?'

Gaff nearly choked on his pint. 'Christ, Dave, I weren't expecting you. So sorry I never…'

'Yeah yeah, never mind that old toffee, Charlotte's in trouble.'

'Chris's Charlotte?'

'Chris's ex?'

'Yeah, never mind him. We need to pay some cunt a visit. Are you in?'

The two Mods exchanged a look.

'Yeah, I'm in,' said Billy, downing the remnants of his pint.

'Lead on MacDuff,' said Gaff, hitting the fruit machine one last time, and winning £15.

'Mac-Who?'

'Never mind. We're in.'

***

Just after 6pm, three scooters were parked up outside a deserted Highgate mews. Dave had dismounted and removed his helmet before the engine was even turned off. He was keen. Ready for action. Whoever was in charge of rehabilitation at the Scrubs had done a shit job.

Dave was pleasantly surprised to see Chris a few yards away.

'Where have you been? I came on the bus. I've been here bleedin' ages.'

Dave shook his hand.

'I knew you do the right thing. Come on! The gang's all here.'

The street was cobbled and deserted without a nosey neighbour to be seen.

'It's down there,' Chris nodded. 'The green door. Number 3.'

Dave took the slip of paper from his pocket and nodded. 'Yep. Three it is.'

Dave was like a man on a mission. Chris felt a little unsettled at how desperate his pal was to get back to the business of bovver. He barely had the smell of jail off him and yet here he was, ready to put the boot in to some geezer he had never even seen. This was no act of gentlemanly honour to protect Charlotte's good name, just a desire for violence. Plain and simple.

'What's the plan then?' said Gaff as he took off his helmet and sat it on the seat of his scooter.

'Plan?' snorted Dave indignantly. 'We knock seven shades of shit out of the cunt and get Charlotte's gear back. It's not fucking *Raid on Entebbe*.'

He rapped on the door loudly and the sound of knuckles on wood echoed round the quiet street. Chris stepped closer to the door and puffed his chest out a bit.

'I'll deal with this bastard,' he said firmly.

Dave just laughed dismissively and banged on the woodwork again. They all stood silently for about twenty seconds but the door remained firmly closed, until Dave stepped back and booted just above the keyhole with the base of his foot. The sound of splintering wood echoed loudly and the door swung inwards.

'Oh look,' said Dave as he made his way inside, 'It was open all along.'

Although it looked like a quaint Victorian abode from the outside, Halpin's pad was just a huge white-washed space inside. Any structure that was not holding the roof up had been removed and the walls were covered in large black & white framed photographs. Chris nearly gasped in grudging awe of Halpin's ultra-modern interior design.

There was an unmade bed near a window, and a well-worn Chesterfield couch provided the only seating other than the large garishly-coloured cushions and bean bags that were scattered across the floor. The rest of the room was awash with sculptures, African figures in dark wood and a 1950s fag machine that was bolted to the wall.

'Over here,' said Chris, pointing to the small pile of Charlotte's belongings that had just been cast aside next to a coffee percolator in the corner of the room that passed for a kitchen. The old lothario had just kept hold of them for spite. Chris strode across the room to retrieve her purse and bits and bobs.

'Right, we've got what we came for, let's shoot,' he said. Chris turned and made for the door but Dave blocked his exit.

'Are you fucking joking?' he sneered. 'This cunt has got it coming. Charlotte's a mate of mine as well remember.' Chris was sure Dave couldn't give him Charlotte's surname if his life depended on it, but he sensed that that was the only excuse his mate needed to justify what he knew was coming next. Dave was primed and ready to inflict damage and obviously as the old perv photographer wasn't there to receive his punishment then it looked like his fixtures and fittings were going to get it instead.

Dave noticed with glee that a Stanley knife and some packing materials were piled up on a paint-spattered work bench near the front window. He grabbed the blade and slashed viciously at the antique couch. Horse hair piled up on the carpet as the worn leather was cut to ribbons.

'Hold up,' said Gaff with a greedy glint in his eye. 'Some of this gear has got to be worth a bob or two. I know a geezer up Brick Lane that might give us something for a few prime pieces of arty tat.'

'Take what you want,' roared Dave as he dropped the knife down on what had been a couch.

'And the rest?' whispered Billy who was feeling a strong desire for devastation building up inside him. Dave laughed. He picked up a heavy glass ashtray and launched it at one of the framed prints on the wall.

'What do you think?' he replied.

As his friends started to lay waste to the room, Chris stared at the bed. The scene of the crime so to speak. Right where his sweet Charlotte had been conned out of her underwear by that sleazy old bastard. His impatience to leave dissipated like dew on a sunny day. He felt hate, rage and something else raged deep in his stomach – a gnawing, churning feeling that rumbled deep in his bowels. He knew he had something to get off his chest but failing that something out of his arse would do. Amidst the chaos of his friends' reign of destruction Chris Davis stood on the bed, dropped his Levi's and parked a sizeable shit on Halpin's pillow.

'smears on your pillow, a pain from my arse, all caused by you…' as the song almost certainly didn't go…

***

8pm. Canning Town.

With Dave out and about with Gaff seeking a fence for the only unbroken art items that had been left in Halpin's smashed up pad, Chris took a shower and enjoyed some early evening peace. It looked like his little flat would no longer be a place of sanctuary until Dave found a place of his own, so he was making the most of it.

Suddenly the new-found tranquillity was rudely shattered by a banging on his front door. Cursing, Chris left the shower running and wrapped a towel around his waist as he plodded along the hall to see who it was, leaving a trail of wet footprints on the lino. Happy days! It was Debbie, looking especially fetching in a dog-tooth mini-skirt and a tight Fred Perry that left little to the imagination.

The effect was so immediate that Chris had to reposition his damp towel to semi conceal the evidence, or should that be evidently conceal the semi?

'Are you in?' said Debbie, unleashing a glorious smile that seemed to light up the hallway.

'I think I am,' he laughed ushering her into the flat like a doorman at the Ritz. They kissed in the tight hallway, which did nothing to curtail the stirring under Chris's towel.

'I'll just finish off and get dressed,' he said quietly when they eventually broke out of their lip lock.

'Okay, tiger.'

He left her walking into the living room and strode back to the shower. The boner was fully fledged now. Should he sort it out quickly now, he pondered? Probably a bad idea. He reached for the temperature knob, hoping that a burst of cold water would literally cool his ardour. But suddenly the shower curtain was pulled back and Debbie was standing there in front of him completely starkers.

'Mind if I join you?' she whispered. She didn't wait for an answer, she just stepped in beside him and started to kiss him. He responded and the kisses became greedier and more urgent. Chris let his soapy hands run wild over her smooth back, and then dropped them down to caress her arse cheeks. She did the same to him and then at pretty much the same time both of them let their fingers stray round to the front. She grasped his cock and held it firmly and then gasped as his fingers progressed to the edges of heaven – her 'Jack and Danny', as the club comics say. Slowly and gently, he let a solitary finger push into the moistness of her and probe deeper.

The whole scene was like something straight out of the letters' pages of Fiesta, he thought. Then another thought occurred. He'd never shagged a bird standing up in a shower. Why not now?

Chris took away his finger and bent his knees slightly so that he could introduce his old chap to the party. His cock was positioned directly under the entry point, and he pushed forward, so it felt like he was shagging her undercarriage. How to manoeuvre it in? The primal urge to penetrate her was building but the soap suds and running water weren't helping. He couldn't quite get in the right position to reach his desired destination.

Debbie rested her face on the top of his chest and giggled a little. He felt his face redden but then dismissed the embarrassment. Firstly, this was a maiden voyage so hiccups were inevitable, secondly, a few laughs perfectly complimented this bizarre situation. And if it was good enough for Robin Askwith, then it was fine with him.

Eventually Debbie provided the solution by sliding up her left leg to accommodate him. Jackpot! The pounding began immediately. The laughter subsided and they both descended into primitive grunting for the duration.

***

Ten minutes later, Chris sat on the edge of the bed in a partial post-coital stupor. He had managed to dry himself off and pull on a clean pair of pants, but the effort had exhausted him and he had to take a breather. He had only really known Debbie for four days and already she was right at the top of his 'best shags ever' list. He couldn't believe how quickly things had developed and a goofy grin was spread right across his boat. The smile evaporated as soon as he heard a knock at the door as he was sure it was Dave, back to spoil the party.

He swung the door open to see someone much prettier.

'Hi Chris,' said Charlotte.

Oh shit! For once in his life Chris Davis was lost for words. His ex-girlfriend was there, and she looked fabulous – she had clearly got herself together and no longer looked like the tear-stained, slightly grubby girl that she had been sobbing in his flat earlier in the day.

She actually looked as if she was ready for a night on the town with full make-up and her barnet combed meticulously; she was wearing in a tight black leather mini-skirt and silky white blouse.

Chris's heart pogoed. She looked so hot, but – and this is where it all went to shit – if Charlotte had come over for a romantic reunion, then she was in for a shock. Even he knew that the chances of some kind of erotic fantasy three-way split occurring imminently, or indeed at all, was about as likely as Bolton not getting relegated. His mind raced, but a good excuse to terminate their conversation evaded him. So Chris held the door ajar, neither shutting it nor inviting her in. She frowned, more than a little put out by his apparent lack of warmth.

'I just wondered if you had any luck over at Harold's?' she continued, as Chris continued to just stare at her blankly. 'My purse and jewellery? Did you find them?'

'Yeah, yeah,' Chris mumbled, his mind still racing to find a solution to this potentially disastrous situation.

'Can I come in then?'

There was a slight hint of anger in her voice.

'I'm not dressed.'

She gave him a look.

'Yeah, sure.'

He quickly made his way into the living room to retrieve Charlotte's belongings, maybe if he moved quickly enough, he could hand it all over and get shot of her without either of the women being aware of the other's presence. In fairness, he had every right to be seeing Debbie. Charlotte had fucked off with the perv. She'd cheated on him and then dumped him. In poker terms, he had a Royal Flush. Any bloke would agree. But bird logic was a whole different can of worms. She'd probably be double furious that a) he hadn't been devastated by her leaving and b) he'd barely let his bed cool down before putting another Richard to the pork sword. So he had to get her in and out like the SAS.

Some chance!

'Ain't you got any bigger ones than this, lover boy?' asked Debbie as she strolled into the room clad only in a towel that barely covered her privates.

'Oh,' she said as she noticed Charlotte standing in front of her with a shocked expression. 'I didn't know we had company.'

Chris let his mouth sag open slightly as he fruitlessly fumbled for the right words. Luckily, he didn't have to say a dicky bird. Charlotte grabbed the purse from his hands, and then turned around and stormed out with fresh tears welling in her eyes.

'Avon Lady?' giggled Debbie, as she headed back to the bathroom leaving Chris alone in his underpants.

***

Chris spent most of the day dazed and slightly confused. The good news was firstly Dave didn't seem to be bearing a grudge, with time their relationship would be back to how it was; and secondly he was genuinely chuffed that he had this thing with Debbie who was as funny as she was tough and definitely up for it anyway, anyhow, anywhere he chose – someone should write a song about that, he mused, oh yeah, they had. The Who's lyrics rocked around his brain, '*Don't care anyway, I never lose, anyway, anyhow, anywhere I choose*'. Debbie was a keeper for sure.

The bad news was all Charlotte. Despite the heartache she'd put him through he was genuinely sorry that she had found out about Debbie the way she had, and gutted that she was so obviously wrecked by the cruel realisation that she couldn't just waltz back into his life and his bed.

She still loved him. It should please him, but there is such a thing as too much choice. He daydreamed about a scenario where he'd kept both of them on the go – as if he'd have the energy. But neither of these women were the bit-on-the-side type. They were all-or-nothing girls – the way he liked them.

Bored of the local pubs, Chris and Debbie had headed into Soho for a mooch and then strolled down to the Embankment and took a chance that there might be more going on south of the river. By 7pm they were in The Wellington at Waterloo where Barney & The Rubbles were due to play later. Chris wasn't too sure how they'd go down with Debbie. The Rubbles weren't strictly a Mod band, more West Ham lunatics with rudimentary musical skills and Barney's unusual poems. But at least they'd made some effort to celebrate St George's Day – an England flag over the drum kit. Have it!

Deborah had popped to the ladies so he got a round in. Lager top for him, gin and slim for her. Chris spotted Barney at the other end of bar and gave him a nod. They didn't know each other to speak to, but they recognised each other from the Upton Park West Side. The hardcore mob. Barney knew Dave. Well, who didn't?

He sat down at a corner table as Debbie walked back.

'I meant to tell you, do you fancy coming to a party next weekend?' she said.

'A Mod one?'

'Family. I told my uncle Steve all about you and he said to bring you. I told him about Dave too. He likes the sound of both of you.'

'This is the Mod uncles, yeah?'

'Yeah, the ones I told you about. Original sixties Mods. Proper East End. Self-made men.'

'And they are also the bollock-whacking uncles?'

'Yeah. Bollocks whacked, knees capped, legs broken.'

'What was their surname again?'

She answered 'Knight', but the name was drowned by a burst of heavy guitar. KERRANG! The Rubbles had started their soundcheck with a power-chord, a wail of feedback and Barney Rubble intoning the lyrics to Bootboys. Debbie cringed. She leaned forward and shouted into Chris's ear.

'They're not Mod then?'

'Not even close.'

'Come on, let's get some grub.'

'Okay.'

They downed their drinks in one and left the pub. Shame, thought Chris. He wouldn't have minded seeing them play. It was usually a good atmosphere there, with little firms of Mods from all over London having it large.

'Shall we go to The Cut for pie and mash?' asked Debbie. 'Good English food for our patron saint's day.'

'I think they shut at six. Let's ham roll down towards the Elephant. There's bound to be a fish and chip shop open.'

'Or a Chinese… I like a bit of chow mein.'

'What happened to good English food?'

'Well if no one can be arsed to do a proper St George's Day show, why should I miss out on a bit of wok and spring roll?'

'Is a duck out of the question?'

'I'm not answering that.'

'I can cover you in orange sauce and lick it off. Slowly.'

'Nice idea, but you're mixing up continents. Orange sauce is French, the Chinese use hoisin?'

'Oi what?'

'Give us a kiss.'

Once they'd started, they couldn't stop. They walked down Waterloo Road towards the Elephant & Castle, pausing every twenty yards or so for a snog. They reached the first bus stop and Chris pulled her under the shelter for a longer one, relishing the feel of her body pressed hard against his as their tongues made like conger eels.

Loved up, pre-occupied and way off his manor, Chris had failed to notice a gang of tearaways who had been following them for the last 100yards.

'Oi,' said one. Chris looked up and saw five blokes, most of them about his age. Two black, two white, one mixed race. They weren't Mods or soul boys. They were just normal. A street gang in shit clothes.

'All right?' he said, knowing full well they weren't.

'We will be,' said the mixed-race boy. 'When you turn your pockets out.'

'Yeah,' said the smaller of the white blokes. 'You're off your manor, son. We need to tax ya.'

Chris thought the creep looked like Disney's lost dwarf, but then he noticed a glint of sharp metal in his hand and realised he was no kids' cartoon.

'We're Millwall,' Chris lied.

'We don't give a fuck about football,' said the dwarf with the blade.

'Empty your pockets you flash cunt,' a lanky black youth said sternly, in a voice like Barry White gargling gravel. He also produced a flick-knife, which he waved menacingly in their direction.

Chris and Debbie both pushed back against the bus shelter. There was no way out of this. For fuck's sake, thought Chris as he struggled to take it all in. Not another mugging in a matter of days? Outside of the bedroom, his luck was poxed. He was just relieved that he'd hidden Barton's stash back at the flat or these bastards would have hit the jackpot.

'Your cash, your watch,' spat the short white youth. 'Hand it over or I'll open you up like a can of beans, you fucking mug.'

Chris hesitated. Bruce Lee could have taken all these jokers out in under thirty seconds, and Chris thought that he'd have a good chance with each of them individually. But there was no way on earth he could knock out five tooled-up hooligans on his tod. He wasn't match fit, and if he let Debbie get involved, she could get really hurt.

'Fight or flight' wasn't an option. They couldn't run, and they couldn't win a tear-up. He sighed. No way out. But as Chris's hand reached for his wallet, he noticed that the second white geezer – who was clearly a few years older than the others – was now eyeing up Debbie.

Don't let him make a move on her, thought Chris, or I'll have to steam in.

He made mental calculations. He reckoned he could knock out two of the cunts before he got plunged, and maybe have enough adrenalin flowing through him to chin a third. That would leave Debbie against two, who might also be carrying. Better odds but still not good enough to take the risk.

His heart sank as he saw the older white man move towards the mixed-race bloke, who held himself like he was the leader, and whispered something unintelligible in his ear. Slowly the bloke's knife hand dropped to his side. He ignored the wallet in Chris's outstretched hand and he looked straight at Debbie.

'I am really sorry, no disrespect,' the youth said quietly. He looked embarrassed. No, more than that, he looked ashamed.

'Sorry,' he said again. 'We're all sorry. This shouldn't have happened. Enjoy your night.'

His shoulders drooped and he gestured at the rest of his firm to get moving. Then he stopped and added quietly, 'If you have any ag around here getting wherever you're going, just tell them you are friends of Marcus Neill. You won't have any more problems. My life.'

As they disappeared into the darkness Chris looked at Debbie for an explanation.

'What the fuck was that?'

'I've no idea,' she said with a shrug, and then she burst into quick bout of giggles. 'Maybe my beauty tamed the savage beast,' she laughed.

'Well, I'm sure it could, but no, this wasn't that Deb – that older geezer knew you. He clocked you.'

'Can't say I knew him, unless he's materialised from a bad dream.'

Chris thought for a minute and then said, 'What did you say your uncle Steve's surname was again?'

'Knight.'

'Wait. Steve Knight. And the other uncle is...'

'Kenny.'

'You serious? Steve and Kenny Knight? The Knights! They're your fucking uncles.'

'Last time I looked.'

'But they're huge.'

'That's just middle-aged spread.'

'Fuck me Debbie. You could have told me sooner. They're like underground royalty.'

'They're me uncles. They're normal blokes.' She paused and winked. 'Until you cross 'em.'

'Fucksake. I probably need a permit to kiss you, let alone, y'know...'

She laughed. 'Yeah, you'd definitely need to be talking rings before they'd let you fuck me. If they knew your filthy intentions, words would be had.'

Chris stared at her with a mix of awe and desire.

'I've gone off grub, shall we go home?'

'Okay. They've still got chinkies in Canning Town haven't they?'

'One or two that won't have been robbed.'

'Good. I don't wanna get the bus though.'

Chris looked up the road and spotted a black cab.

'Taxi!'

'Flush,' she said.

'Well I never lost me wallet, did I. I'd written this cockle off.'

The cab pulled up and he opened the door for her.

'Canning Town, please driver. Through the pipe. Up by the fly-over.'

The driver grunted.

'If it's more than a tenner, I'm paying half. No argument.'

He reached out for her hand and, as he felt her soft fingers entwine with his, all his thoughts of the muggers and of Charlotte slipped away like shit off a hot shovel.

7

Thursday 24th of April, 1980

'This place is a fucking pigsty,' said Gaff as he rooted around on the littered coffee table in Chris's living room. 'Seriously Chris. It really went downhill when Charlotte fucked off.'

'Most of that shit is her leftovers,' yelled Chris from the kitchen where he stood waiting for the kettle to boil.

Gaff continued to flick through all the old *Maximum Speed* fanzines and old copies of *Sounds* that were gathering dust.

'Messy, Mr Davis, very messy,' he mocked. 'And not very Mod. I thought my drum was bad and it's like something from *Animal House*. I thought you'd be able to tidy things up seeing as you seem to be a gentleman of leisure these days.'

'I'm going back to work,' protested Chris as he walked through with two mugs of coffee and sat down. 'I've just missed a few days. I'll get a note from the quack. I thought I might as well wait until these bruises on my boat have faded a bit. I was meant to have some kind of appraisal this week and I didn't want to turn up like Henry Cooper after his second dance with Ali. Anyway, you've got a fucking cheek. When did you last do an honest day's graft?'

'Leave it out,' roared Gaff. He took a long slurp of coffee and went on in mock outrage, 'How dare you? I'm in the import/export game – a self-made man, crafted in the white heat of Maggie's post-socialist Britain. My mum says I could sell ice to the Eskimos and cages to lions. And you know what, Chrissy Boy?' He patted the pocket of his suit jacket. 'I've been doing some ducking and diving this morning in fact. Talking of which, fancy a little acid trip to make the day seem brighter?'

'Fuck off,' spluttered Chris. 'You're not doing LSD as well now, are you? I thought it was just the Billy Whizz that you flogged. It's a slippery slope mate, soon you'll be hanging outside the school gates punting smack. Total mug's game.'

'All right, all right, Norman Tebbit, keep yer hair on. It's just a one-off. Once I've flogged these tabs, I'm out of it.'

'You'd be out of it if you took them.'

'Listen, I'll be glad to be shot of them, to be honest, not many of our lot want to *kiss the sky*. Here did Billy tell you about that bird he pulled last night?'

Chris shock his head.

'Gorgeous but a fuckin' bedroom disaster. Fanny like a bucket. He said it was like that Stranglers song, 'Making love to the Mersey Tunnel…'

'With a sausage!'

Both of them sang the last line together, '*Have you ever been to Liverpool?*'

'Where was this?'

'Long Tall Shorty gig last night.'

'How was it?'

'A lot like the song, large venue, small enthusiastic crowd that didn't quite touch the sides. Good gig though.'

'Tony's always good. I was with Debbie.'

Chris told him the whole story, including the bus stop trauma and Debbie's family background.

'The Knights? Shit. That's serious fuckery right there. And you're having a pop at me for flogging a bit of

Leary!' He pondered for a moment and added casually, 'So where's Charlotte now?'

'Out of the picture.'

Gaff's face lit up. 'So she's a free agent. I wouldn't mind a go on that. Would you mind?'

Mind, thought Chris, of course I'd fucking mind. 'Not at all,' he said coolly. 'We're over.' Chris took a sip of coffee and wondered when he'd see Debbie next. Gaff nodded happily and picked up the latest issue of *Sounds*. But as he did so, he knocked a Xeroxed flyer on the floor.

'What's this then?' he said, as he picked it up. 'Oh mate, bingo! This is the place. What day is it?'

'Thursday. I think.'

'Thursday 24th! Fucking brilliant. Look at this.' Gaff thrust a crudely photocopied flyer towards Chris – it was something Charlotte had been given at one of her arty-farty parties and simply said *Night For Heroes* along with an address in Warren Street. The date and the words '*Dress fabulous*' were the only other information on it.

'Looks like some poncey art do,' said Chris contemptuously.

'No mate, it looks like exactly the place where we want to be. In amongst all the freaks. Most of those posh cunts are loaded as well. Little rich kids raiding the dressing-up box. I can flog these trips for sure.'

Chris sucked his lips as his thoughts automatically went straight to Charlotte again. Maybe she'd be there? Did he want to see her? He wanted to take Debbie but he didn't want another scene. That would be seen as rubbing Charlotte's nose in it. If she kicked off, Debbie might deck her. Bollocks. Ifs and maybes make no babies.

'Yeah, I'm up for it. What about Billy and Dave?'

'Billy will come for sure, he'll need to get his confidence back after last night's trip to 'the Cavern'. It'd be good to take the jailbird as well. It'd be an act of charity. The only action he's seen in the past year is a poke up the jacksy in the shower block.'

Chris shrugged. 'Not sure where he's got to, but I'll tell him if I see him.'

He hadn't seen much of his unwanted new flatmate since the Halpin escapade. All he had heard recently was the front door bang as Dave went out.

'What's going on with him?' asked Gaff. 'He went fucking nuts smashing up Halpin's flat and after we flogged that gear, he just took his share of the cash and pissed off.'

'Maybe he's giving us the silent treatment. He's still got the hump about prison visits. He thinks we just cut him off.'

Gaff laughed that off. 'Fuck him, he's always been a moody cowson anyway.' He slammed the empty mug down and grabbed the flyer back out of Chris's grip. 'Right! I'll speak to Billy and I'll meet you outside the Post Office at eight. Until then I'm heading home for a wank, a kip and then a wash and brush up.'

'Cheers for sharing that,' said Chris sarcastically.

'It's a ham shank for most of us brother,' said Gaff as he opened the front door. 'We can't all bounce about between two stunners like you do.'

***

It had not been hard to persuade Billy to accompany them to the 'posh pricks dressing-up party' and as they drove along Warren Street, Gaff pulled out the flyer to confirm the exact address. He and Billy were on their own scooters; Chris had Debbie sitting behind him on his. Chris had taken a fair bit of stick about been pussy-whipped for bringing her along but he didn't give a fuck. At least he had a bird, and a bloody good one at that.

He hated 'pussy-whipped' as a term of abuse as well, he preferred to think of himself as *blinded by beaver*.

Gaff signalled for them to pull up near a large four storey townhouse but it was pretty obvious that they were in the right place. Gangs of wackily dressed punters were already hanging around outside and some flashing lights and music emanated from the building. They parked up on the opposite side of the street. There was a fairly tatty Vincent Black Shadow motorbike parked a few doors up.

'Grease?' asked Billy as he removed his helmet.

'Nah,' sneered Gaff. 'Probably some toff boy done up in all the Marlon Brando clobber. A weekend *Wild One*.'

'But it's only Thursday…' joked Billy weakly.

Chris helped Debbie off the scooter and they started to walk over to the house.

'Do you think we'll need an invite,' he said as they got closer.

'Bit late to wonder now,' she laughed.

Gaff waved the flyer triumphantly. 'This is all we need, that and my infinite personal charm of course.'

'Charm?' sniped Chris. 'Christ, we're fucked.'

Any optimism Chris had dissolved the moment they got to the door. Holding fort was a tall skinny dipstick of a geezer with ridiculously backcombed hair, and what looked like a piece of modern art painted on his face. Resplendent in full Lawrence Of Arabia clobber and knee-high brown leather boots, he stood there like an immovable object at the entrance.

'Not tonight, boys,' he preened imposingly.

Gaff stepped closer and whispered something in his ear his tone changed immediately.

'Apologies, apologies. Come one, come all,' he roared in a high-camp tone. 'Nice boys, clean boys… and a dolly

little devotchka. Welcome to the garden of dark delights.'
And they were in.

'What did you tell him?' asked Billy.

'Need to know, mate, need to know.'

***

After a few hours Chris realised how right he was to have
invited Debbie. Without her, he would have been bored
out of his tits. After the initial shock of seeing all the
pretty things poncing about, though the novelty had
worn off, he realised how deadly dull they were. Sure, as
a Mod, he did have a grudging respect for anyone who
chose a sartorially challenging subculture to tie their flag
to, but this scene in particular was not for him. It just
seemed like pantomime to him, the people were
horrendous ponces – not least the cunt from Carry On
Camel at the front door – and the music was beyond
garbage. He could just about stomach the old Bowie and
Roxy Music records that were getting an airing but the
screechy sub-Kraftwerk electronic stuff put his teeth on
edge.

As he sat with Debbie on an old couch that had
obviously been rescued from a skip, Chris quickly
scanned the room for Charlotte. He didn't really want to
meet her, not when he was with Debbie of course, but
she was a hard woman to forget so quickly; and of course
the revelation that she still had a thing for him was a turn-
on, even though it would be suicidal to act on it. Or at
least extremely damaged to his cojones…

He looked over at Debbie and got a warm thrill again
just seeing how damn hot she looked. Better *a bird in the
hand* as they say.

Gaff was working the room as usual and he seemed to
be on demand for his chemical wares, while Billy looked

to have pulled a statuesque blonde with pink tints and unusual but not unpleasant features. Debbie noticed Chris looking over and nudged him in the ribs.

'See something you like do you?'

'Eh? No, I was just looking at that bird Billy is with and wondering why his mush looks like something you'd see back in a hall of mirrors. Fit woman in every other sense but her Chevvy is making me feel cross-eyed.'

'Don't get too excited watching her, darling. I reckon he's in for a shock.'

'How do you mean?'

'Take a better look at *her*. I reckon there's a dangling pair of balls under that PVC skirt.'

'Fuck off. You're having a laugh. She's all woman by the looks of it.'

'Oh yeah? Look again. A bit too much all woman in my opinion. The hair, the size 12 plates, the slap that looks like it's been trowelled on by a plasterer… I reckon if Billy puts his hand up that skirt he's going to find something dangling to grab on to with balls attached to the end and not church bells.'

'Oh if he gets that far I don't think it'll be dangling,' laughed Chris. 'It'll be standing to attention like a Grenadier guardsman on fucking parade.'

She laughed. 'Still she's done a good job on the pins, very waxy.'

'Shaved her legs and then he was a she…'

'Doo do doo do doo do do doo…'

They laughed but their joy was short-lived. A hairy biker suddenly staggered across the room and fell down onto the spare seat next to Debbie, making her spill her can of Breaker all down her top.

'Oi, watch what you're doing you greasy bastard,' she yelled.

'Shut the fuck up, you dirty brass, it's the only seat in the house.' Chris leapt to his feet like the bell had just gone for round one and shot over to where the stoned biker was sitting. Without pausing for breath, he hit him straight on the nose, which broke on impact creating a fountain of blood. Bam! He followed it with three kick punches to his jaw, his right temple and his left eye. Bam! Bam! Bam!

The dazed hairy was teetering on the verge of consciousness. Claret was cascading down his face and dripping all over his no-longer-white Saxon t-shirt. Chris grabbed him firmly by his leather jacket, dragged him up from the seat and sent him spinning down the hallway and out the door. A couple who saw it gasped in horror, but those who saw merely the aftermath barely blinked an eye. They no doubt imagined the brief but violent fracas was some high-end form of street theatre.

It was only when Chris returned to his seat on the other side of Debbie, collapsing onto the settee, that he could feel the shooting pain in his knuckles.

'What the fuck was all that about?' said Gaff.

'Your weekend Wild One, mate,' said Chris, rubbing his knuckles. 'Slagged off Debbie and soaked her with beer.'

'Oh, my hero,' twittered Gaff in a high-pitched cold Georgia accent as he flapped an imaginary fan. Then they both laughed loudly.

'This is the fucking place, bruv,' said Gaff. 'I've flogged all the acid and most of the speed. They can't get enough of it.'

'Can we go then? This shit-hole place is doing my nut in.'

'New directions, new sensations mate, that's what it's meant to be about ain't it?'

Gaff gave a dry laugh.

'There ain't nothing new about some cunt dressed like he's auditioning for the fuckin' Wild One. And as for the rest of them, it's like *Tomorrow's World* for nonces.'

Gaff laughed. 'It's okay with me, Chris, I've done the lot and I'm holding folding. But I reckon you might have a harder job convincing Billy to leave, than me. Have a pipe at that!'

They all looked over to see their mate who was locked together at the lips with the tall blonde. The pair of them were really going at it. His hands were sliding all over her body, while her hands massaged his chest firmly before moving up and gripped him tightly around the neck.

'Is she trying to fucking strangle him?' asked Gaff. 'Oi love, it's his chicken your supposed to choke.'

'Oh this is fucking funny,' said Chris. 'I suppose we can't leave now, not with Lola getting fruity.'

'Lola? Is that her name?'

'No,' laughed Debbie. 'It's a song.'

Gaff went blank for a moment and then the penny dropped.

'You mean, that's a… geezer? For fuck's sake. Shall we tell him?'

'What? Before he finds out? Where's the pleasure in that?'

'It's Pinky,' said Debbie.

'What is?'

'The tranny's name. I heard someone say "Hello Pinky" earlier.'

'You seen any beer, Gaff? I'm parched.'

'I'll have a scout around.'

Five minutes later, Gaff found a fridge and purloined a six-pack of Stella to keep them going. Chris took one greedily and downed it in two gulps.

'Where are the love birds?'

'Love berks. They went that way.' Chris pointed to the stairs. 'They went up.'

The three Mods went up one floor, and then another. There was a small box room with the door shut. Gaff took a chance, eased it open and saw a scene he could never unsee.

He turned to the others. 'It's going down on him.'

'Let's see,' said Debbie. She peeked around the door and pulled back. 'Ooh, nice technique.'

'He is going to be so pissed off,' said Chris.

'Shall we put a stop to it? I'd hate him to grope Pinky and find a perky surprise.'

'We could be at home doing that,' moaned Chris.

'Well, come on then, I've had enough of this. The music is proper shite, and the people are dull. Let's go, You should get Billy, Gaff, before the inevitable happens.'

She was right, thought Chris. The music was shite and it kept getting louder. Right now there was some low rumble that was even drowning out Gary Numan or whatever the fuck crap was playing. It got louder and louder. Then he realised it was coming from outside. Chris looked out of the window.

'Fuck. Gaff, get Billy.'

'What is it?'

'Bikers! Fucking loads of them by the looks of it.' They had to be mates of the cunt he'd thrown out, otherwise it was one hell of a coincidence. 'Get Billy.'

Gaff kicked open the door. 'Bill we've gotta go!'

'What? Why? I'm with this Richard.'

'You don't wanna be, mate. No time to explain. We need to find an escape route pronto.'

They headed down to the floor below, with Billy jamming his erection into his pants and doing up his flies. Nobody was taking any notice of the noise outside. They went down another floor and SMASH! A brick came sailing through the window hitting a bloke with blue lipstick and a floor-length leather overcoat in the head.

That got their attention! Most of them squealed and three women ran to assist the bleeding poser on the floor.

'Send out those fucking Mods or we're coming in to get them,' came a rough voice from outside. The party-going posers almost spun round as one to clock Chris, Gaff, Debbie and Billy, but no one made any move to eject them. A second brick followed, shattering through another window and forced the fledgeling new romantics into action.

'Come on, Butch, time to go,' said a hulking drag queen as he tried to pull Chris towards the hall.

'Back off,' growled Chris, shaking off the man's grip.

'I don't think so.' The drag queen pulled out a kitchen knife from some inexplicable part of his sequinned ballgown. 'You and your mates. Out! Fucking move it.'

'Who are you, Danny La Rude?'

That was pretty good for me, thought Chris. He stayed rooted to the spot, keeping an eye on the blade as he tried to work out the best way to dispose of the threat, until Billy's voice broke the stalemate.

'Chris. Debs. Over here.' He was gesturing towards a door at the back of a room, where he was being dragged towards by the blonde girl who he didn't know wasn't a girl. The rest of the gang followed him and soon they had pushed their way through the crowd and escaped out the back door, bursting out into a cramped back garden. It was no more than four yards long and was overshadowed by an office block that cut out much of the fairly minimal street light that seeped around the edges of the rooftops. The fences between the garden and the neighbouring properties were either broken or missing altogether, so they made their way through them without too much trouble. Behind them was a cacophony of screams, yells and the unmistakeable sound of fixtures and fittings being reduced to matchwood. The bikers had obviously grown tired of waiting outside and had entered the premises by force.

'Over here,' said Pinky, who pointed at an ancient caravan that had been jammed against the back gate of the last building in the row. It was unlocked. Pinky dragged Billy inside and the rest of them followed, ducking down on the floor. Not exactly The Alamo, thought Chris but it'd have to do. If this was going to be their last stand, at least there would be tools here.

Every moment seemed like a minute and every minute an hour. They listened intently. Less than a hundred yards away, the sound of chaos raged on but none of the dim bikers had thought to try and follow them.

'This is stupid,' hissed Gaff. 'We're like fish in a barrel if they find us here.'

'Shut the fuck up then,' whispered Billy. 'Do you want to climb over that back gate and take your chances with what's on the other side? Just sit tight.'

'What about the scooters?'

'You'll have a hard job riding home with broken legs if they get us,' said Chris.

'He's right, Gaff, let's just wait for a bit.'

They stayed hunched down for what seemed like an eternity and then they felt a slight rocking motion. The stared at each other in the darkness.

'Is there someone outside,' said Chris in a barely audible tone but Debbie nudged him and pointed behind them. Behind a worn curtain at the other end of the caravan they could see Pinky's head bobbing up and down in the region of Billy's legs as he rammed himself against the shed wall and gurned with anticipation of the ecstasy to come.

'Billy, for fuck's sake,' seethed Chris but he got no reply other than some renewed grunting.

'I can't handle this,' he said and crept forward opening the caravan door slightly. The garden was empty. He made his way to the fence and, standing on a tree stump, he could see that the back garden of the house they had left only contained a few New Romantic types smoking and having some type of animated discussion.

The noise of threats and violence had gone, replaced by Gary Numan's drippy 'Down In The Park'. He opened the caravan door with a grin.

'I think it's over.'

Billy let out a huge groan. 'It is now,' he gasped.

After Billy had done his trousers up and given Pinky a lingering kiss goodbye, the Mods scaled the wall next to the caravan and found themselves in a narrow alley. They walked carefully back towards Warren Street, where they had left their scooters.

On the other side of the road, two van loads of the Met's finest had around ten corralled close to the front door of the party house. The ton-up boys noticed their intended prey saunter past, but there was nothing they could do but glare across the road at them.

'Can we pop back via Hackney?' said Gaff.

'Why?'

'I just need to pick up some supplies.'

'I'd rather head home,' grunted Chris.

'It'll put ten minutes on the journey, if that. I'll just be in and out of the place… I'll feel a lot safer with you me, after all of this…'

'Go on then.'

They drove casually pass the grease. It was so easy Chris couldn't resist giving them a sarcastic wave.

***

They drove up through Islington and on through Dalston to a place called Fassett Square near Ridley Road market. The raw fear of getting a thorough pasting from the bikers had long been replaced by elation. They parked up outside a house with no lights on. Gaff dismounted first.

'There's a pub round the corner, the Queen Elizabeth if you want a pint.'

'You said you'd be five minutes,' said Chris, a little testily.

'I will.'

'So we'll wait.'

Gaff shrugged and strode across the square to a house radiating orange-tinged light. All of the properties were sturdy, built in the German gothic style. Meanwhile Billy went into the cultivated garden area in the middle to piss behind a tree, like a dog leaving his scent.

'Will you tell him about Pinky?' asked Debbie, a smile playing around her lips.

'What, and spoil his night? Nah, I'll keep that in reserve. That's good ammo. You never know when it'll come in handy.'

He looked around. 'These drums look ancient. Are they Georgian, d'you think?'

'No. Much older. Victorian. Must be a hundred years old at least, maybe more.'

'Let's see if we can spot a date on any of them, sometimes they have them on plaster slabs.'

Debbie shrugged. 'Okay. All you've got at your flats are "Kilroy wuz ere", "NF" and "West Ham".'

'And "George Davis Is Innocent", don't forget that.'

'How could I? It's unforgettable. Even if he ain't.'

They left the scooters and helmets, and walked along slowly glancing at the houses. It took just over a minute before Chris guided her into the square's green centre for another bout of tonsil tennis.

'Don't get no ideas,' she said with a smile. 'I won't be doing a Pinky on you in the middle of the square. I know what's on your mind, I can see it.'

She grabbed his erection through his trousers and let her teasing fingers run up and down it, before holding the tip and squeezing it.

'Oh Jesus,' he gasped. But then Chris was snapped out of his randy reverie by a distant rumbling noise that was rapidly becoming louder. Something far darker in spirit than Cupid was entering the square.

Bikers. Three of them. Chris pulled Debbie down behind a bush roughly.

'Oi!'

'Sssh.'

They watched three grease ride in, one on a Norton Commando, two on Royal Enfield Bullets.

'They can't be that lot from before,' she said.

'I think they might be. Look.'

The bikers parked up in a semicircle around the scooters, and started looked around, scanning the Square. They were older men, late twenties at least. Two of them were swinging bike chains, the other had a mean looking machete strapped to his leg.

'They're the ones that got away.'

'And they trailed us here?' asked Debbie.

'My guess is one of them was the scout, with two of them hanging back a way behind. We wouldn't have taken no notice of one bike.'

The bikers had spotted something. 'There!' shouted one. It was Billy. The grease gave chase. The machete was now in the third biker's hand. Billy had seen them though. He turned and ran full pelt towards the house with the orange lights that Gaff had gone into and banged loudly on the door.

'You stay, I'd better go help,' Chris said hoarsely.

'Okay, but watch yourselves. These are geezers, and they're not going to fuck about.'

Gaff was inside the house counting out tenners for the LSD he was buying from Stephane, a mixed-race drug dealer from Amsterdam, when the banging started.

'Oh verdomme. That better not be the filth,' said Stephane. He put down his spliff, picked up a baseball bat and opened the door. Billy flew in.

'Shut it, shut it quick,' he shouted. But before Stephane could act, the leading biker kicked the door open putting the Dutchman on his back.

Billy met Gaff on the stairs and they retreated up to the first floor landing. The three bikers stomped up the stairs, weapons drawn. The Mods backed into the toilet but it had no door.

One burly bearded greaser stepped forward.

'You fuckers have put six of our mates behind bars tonight and one in hospital. So we're gonna repay the favour by putting all of you cunts in casualty.'

He stepped forward swinging his chain. Down below Stephane blew a referee's whistle loudly. Almost instantly a 6ft 4 Rastafarian built like a brick shithouse appeared from the bedroom next to the toilet, and a petite blonde, slender and dressed entirely in black started to come down the narrower staircase that led to the loft.

Down below, Chris had come through the front door clutching a freshly ripped three foot tree branch. He noticed the pervading smell of cannabis, a metal sign reading AFCA nailed to the wall, and Stephane halfway up the stairs with a pistol in his hand.

On the first floor, things were getting interesting. 'That's as far as you go,' said the Rasta in a voice that boomed like Barry White in an echo chamber.

'Says who?' snapped the heavy lead bearded biker who had his machete drawn.

'Says me, Sanka,' replied the Rasta who was now holding an AMT AutoMag in his right hand. The slender blonde on the stairs had produced a Beretta. The bikers stopped, did a double take, and took a swift step backwards.

Stephane had appeared on the stairs behind them holding a Heckler & Koch P9, with Chris behind him, still clutching his tree branch.

'Drop your weapons and fuck off,' Stephane commanded.

The bikers reluctantly complied, their improvised metal weapons clattering on the wooden floor like a soundtrack of defeat. They glowered at Stephane, and Chris even more so as they walked down past him, but said nothing. Sanska stayed on the landing, but the blonde followed them down, still clutching her Beretta. She stopped level with Chris, and he couldn't help but soak up her erotic smell, an intoxicating mix of incense, vanilla and Italian bergamot.

'Don't even think about coming back here,' Stephane growled at the bikers. 'If we see any of you in this neighbourhood you'll be shot on sight. Do you understand?'

The lead biker grunted.

'And leave my friends' scooters intact.'

Gaff and Billy looked jubilant.

'Thank you so much, Stephane. That was so fucking cool,' said Gaff.

'Leave this house,' the Belgian barked.

'What? But the deal...?'

'Fuck the deal. You bring trouble to my door. I can't work with you. You're lucky we don't shoot all three of you cunts. Do you understand?'

'I'm so sorry, mate. They've followed us from the West End. We had no idea.'

'I don't give a fuck. Go, and don't come back. You're not welcome here. Take your money and fuck off.'

Gaff held his hands up and for once in his life he had nothing to say. Chris kept quiet, although he exchanged a wordless look with the blonde, who patted his bum as he followed and then flashed a contagious smile.

The three Mods made their way morosely to the scooters, where Debbie was waiting.

'Well, you certainly know how to show a girl a good time,' she quipped. 'A riot at a party, a blow job in a caravan, and the Dukes of fucking Hazzard wandering around East London on a Fuck-a-Mod night-time experience…'

'I'm sorry, babe,' said Chris as he gave her a firm cuddle. He was happy that despite the shit evening she was still joking.

'And on top of all that, while I was waiting for you to stop re-enacting a Mods and Rockers Margate beach battle, I find meself being wanked over by some old hobo.'

'You're joking.'

'I'm not. He was on the floor looking up my skirt with his gnarled old cock in his hand.'

Gaff laughed. 'Well be fair, Deb, you've got cracking pins.'

'Worth wanking over,' agreed Billy.

'Oi!' said Chris, 'show some respect!' He turned to Debbie. 'So where is this dirty perve now?'

'He's sleeping.'

'Sleeping?'

'Yeah, look.' Debbie pointed back into the middle of the square. 'I think the meths must have done it… when I smashed his bottle over his manky head.'

The Mods laughed. This was the life! Well, it was one life at least.

Later that night, in the relative safety of a Canning Town flat, Chris and Debbie shagged slowly and sensuously as if time mattered not one jot. At the crucial moment, he was thinking of the blonde with the Beretta. She definitely wasn't thinking about the tramp.

8

Friday 25th of April, 1980

Chris came to at around 10.30am and reached over for Debbie, unaware that she had already left for work. He melted into an erotic half-doze where he was sharing the bed with Debbie, Charlotte and the petite charmer from the night before. He started to pleasure himself but the mood was shattered by a steady banging on the front door. Debbie, he thought, or maybe Dave. Who else could it be?

'Hold up! Coming!'

He pulled on last night's shirt, just in case it was the old dear from upstairs trying to cadge some sugar. There was no sign of Debbie. She'd obviously remembered what he'd forgotten, he thought, that she was supposed to be at work. The bedside clock said it was gone 11am, way past the acceptable time to phone his work with yet another lame excuse. His week-long adventure was probably stretching any brownie points he had at work to the absolute breaking point. He couldn't lose the job – it was funding the thing that mattered most to him, his Mod lifestyle.

BANG! BANG! BANG!

'For fucksake! Hold on, I am coming!'

He laughed, remembering the many times he'd seen The Chords cover that song live. '*When the day comes and you're down/In a river of trouble and about to drown...*'

He caught sight of Dave lying on the settee smoking a roll-up and remembered getting up in the middle of the night to let him in.

'Are you not hearing this, David?'

'It's your house ain't it? None of my fucking business.'

The banging continued and the letterbox crashed open. A loud Scottish voice boomed out angrily from behind the door, 'Wake up ya English bas! I heard you pumped my sister, you're fuckin' deid.'

'Who the fuck is that?' Chris hissed to Dave who was already off the couch and clutching a hammer. 'Do you sleep with that under your pillow you fucking madman?'

'We might be needing it.'

'It's obviously someone after you mate, I ain't shagged a Jock in months' – actually, a week or so ago, he thought, but who's counting?

'Let me in,' yelled the voice outside. 'I'm going to boot your baws, ya lavvy heid.'

Dave tensed up. Gripping the hammer, he gestured to Chris to open the door and then get out of the way. Chris pulled the door back sharply, steeling himself for some ultraviolence, to find Evvy on his doorstep pissing herself laughing. A large, sharply dressed mod geezer appeared behind her with a beaming smile.

'Morning lads.'

***

The crack of balls on the pool table rattled around the pub, and, despite the early hour, the Horse & Groom on Holloway Road was already enjoying a fair old trade. The lonely, the alcoholic and the desperate made up most of the grey-skinned clientele, but lounging around behind two tables near the back were Dick Barton and his surly mob of soul boys. This was their local and that automatically gave them the right to lord it over the other regulars – plebs! – who knew better than to get in their way.

Although Dick believed it was his own presence that instilled this fear, the truth was that his father's reputation cast a long shadow.

'First of the day,' yelled Johnny as he weaved his way over to the table balancing a tray-full of lagers between his hands.

'Bottoms up,' yelped Little Steve greedily as he lunged for a beer sending a few drops of Carlsberg spilling to the floor and onto Barton's green Adidas Gazelles.

'Easy, you fucking clumsy twat, I paid a fortune for these.'

'No you didn't, Dick,' laughed Pete. 'You fucking half-inched them, same as always, like everything else you're wearing.'

'Either way, I don't want the fuckers soaked in Forsyte Saga just because this arsehole can't hold a pint steady.' He paused and added, 'Heads up!'

Dick's attention was drawn to a powerfully built broad-shouldered bloke who had come into the pub and was wandering about looking the punters up and down like he was looking for someone specific. Dick noticed that the big man wore similar trainers to him, as well as tight jeans and a green flight jacket over a Cockney Rejects t-shirt. His barnet was short, a bit like a skinhead cut that had grown out.

'Who's this cunt? Any idea?' Barton asked. Matt shook his head. 'Never seen him before.'

'I think that's Big Barry Hollis from the Andover estate,' said Pete in little more than a whisper. 'I heard he was away.'

Hollis noticed them and strolled forward, obviously with no intention of buying a drink.

'Who's Barton?' he asked in a flat tone that was neither menacing nor friendly – although Dick thought it was odds on that he knew exactly who he was looking for. Matt, wiry and always game, stood up and tensed, ready for action to protect Dick and give the unknown upstart a good hiding should the need arise.

'Take it easy you mug,' Hollis snapped in a commanding tone. 'I'm only here to deliver a message.'

'I'm Dick Barton,' said Dick, as he reclined casually in his chair like some sawdust Caesar holding court over the hoi polloi.

Hollis nearly smiled. 'I 'eard you got done over by some Mod kids the other day, and they had a little bit of your cabbage as well.'

'Who the fuck told you that?' Barton kicked himself for answering so quickly. He knew he ought to be playing the situation cucumber cool, but the truth was the sting of defeat was still sharp and the cuts and bruises still showed.

'That don't fucking matter,' said Hollis, 'But I do know someone that might be able to help you out.'

'Who? You?' yelped Little Steve aggressively.

'No, not me, you fucking thick dwarf,' Hollis sighed. 'A mate of mine, all right? I don't give a flying fuck if you lot get kicked up and down the streets by Mods, Teds, geisha girls or fairies wearing DM boots to be honest. A mate said he could help and asked me to pass on the message. That's all.'

'Pray tell, Mr... Hollis, was it?' said Barton. 'I'm all ears.' Dick had taken an instant dislike to the stranger, and now realised his instincts had been right. The ice cream was a copper-bottomed cunt. Someone giving them this level of attitude in their own boozer was simply not acceptable, but there was something about the guy and how he held himself that dissuaded him from leaping to his feet, whipping out his Stanley knife and opening the West Ham tosspot up like a can of beans.

Hollis was either ignorant of the Barton family name or he was a complete and utter headcase with a death wish. Either way, it sounded like what he had to say could be of interest – especially if it meant they could get revenge on the muggy Mods and get their cash back pronto.

Hollis looked at him, weighing him up.

'Come on, you've found me. So what's next?'

'Give me your phone number and I'll pass it on,' Hollis replied finally. 'It's best you have a direct conversation, man to man, on the dog.'

'Get a pen, Johnny boy,' ordered Barton.

Johnny went up to the bar and returned with two pens that had obviously been 'borrowed' from the bookies, two doors down. Barton picked up a beermat, scribbled down his home number and passed it over. Hollis looked at it, grunted, and made for the door.

'Goodbye then,' yelled Pete sarcastically.

Hollis just raised a middle finger in the air and carried on walking.

***

Evvy was still laughing as Chris brought through four steaming hot cups of instant coffee into the living room on a worn tea tray. Dave was back on the bed, his trousers were on but he was still glowering at their new visitor. The unknown newbie was Evvy's big brother Stevie, down from Glasgow to stay with her for a bit. The kid had obviously already immersed himself in the Mod scene. Both Dave and Chris had surreptitiously checked out his gear. Stevie was well turned out and if his light-grey Prince of Wales check suit was off the peg, then it was a decent peg. Two and a half inch lapels, ticket pocket, paisley lining... very tasty.

'Two geezers in their underpants looking for a square go,' guffawed Stevie in a broad Glaswegian accent. 'Classic! Welcome to London.'

'Banging on the door like a fucking madman,' growled Dave. 'You nearly got done in.'

'Cheer up ya grumpy cunt,' laughed Stevie. 'We were just having a laugh.'

That kind of comment was usually more than it took for Dave to fly into a Hulk-like rage but like Chris he was still trying to suss out their new visitor. Stevie was a big lump indeed, tall, wide and packing muscle with a fairly fresh six-inch scar down his left cheek. He looked nothing like the diminutive Evvy – maybe their mum had been getting a little something extra from the local milkman. Or if she was anything like her daughter, the full Glasgow Rangers squad, plus the trainer, manager and physios.

'What brought you down here?' asked Chris in an attempt to diffuse the uneasy atmosphere.

'He's down to see what the Mod scene is like here,' interrupted Evvy quickly. 'You lot are always going on about how the big smoke is the centre of it all.'

'Aye, what she said,' agreed Stevie as if that was as good an answer as any.

'So you're staying for a bit?' It was an innocent enough question but coming from Dave it sounded like a challenge.

'Aye, I am,' said Stevie. His voice sounded flatter, as if his initial good humour was starting to fade.

Chris and Evvy tried and steer the conversation in a lighter direction but Dave's continuing sullen bad attitude reeked like turds on the pavement on a hot day. Even an hour later, when Evvy and her brother got up to leave, Stevie and Dave were still giving each other the evil eye.

'See yous both soon,' said Chris cheerily as he shut the door. But his expression changed when he spun round to face Dave.

'What the fuck was all that about? Giving that geezer the big 'un? He seemed all right. What's wrong with you?'

'Flash porridge-munching bastard,' mumbled Dave.

'It's Evvy's brother for fuck's sake. Not some toerag off the street.'

'He started it,' said Dave weakly. 'Banging on the door... shouting.'

Chris had nothing to add. It was always the same with Dave. Leading them all into one scrap after another. It was fucking pointless in most cases. He was a good guy to have on your side if there were other mobs trying to have a pop but mostly it was Dave's attitude that led to confrontations in the first place. Besides, he had enough bovver on his own to deal with. Getting taxed by Dick Barton was bad enough but that bad blood was far from over and that train ride home from Margate with Debbie with all the brutal sub *The Warriors* encounters still haunted his nightmares. In truth he enjoyed the vicarious thrill of random violence and had almost developed a taste for it – beating the bikers had been epic. But the downsides were they had reached a level where people were wielding guns, and when he looked at Dave he realised that going down that same belligerent road was a one-way trip to a dead end.

Dave had been fighting all his life, lashing out at anyone and everyone, but where had it got him? Kipping on his mate's couch with the same Y-fronts on for three days and keeping a hammer under the pillow. If there was any glamour to violence then it had passed Dave by.

There were gigs coming up that Chris wanted to enjoy – the Small Hours at the Bridgehouse, a new band called the Glory Boys at The Wellington... and he wished now he'd gone up to Birmingham a couple of weeks ago to see Secret Affair at the Odeon because they had no other shows this entire summer. Point was, Chris Davis could and would have a row if he needed to, but surely there had to more to life than bashing punks, skins and Millwall.

***

Gaff walked into the record store and felt at home as always. Gaff loved vinyl. In truth, he wasn't real much of a dancer but he hoovered up records greedily and his love for music was, almost, as overwhelming as his desire to make a quick buck. Sure, Billy and Chris attempted to keep up with the music, although Dave only seemed to like being a Mod as an excuse to batter anyone that wasn't one, but Gaff was different. He knew everything about the Mod scene – its roots, its evolution and all the bands that were springing up. Most of the so-called rock press couldn't see beyond The Jam and Quadrophenia, but at least The Chords, the Purple Hearts and Secret Affair were getting positive coverage in *Sounds*. Even the half-wits on daytime radio could just about manage the odd new Mod track – if 'You Need Wheels' by the The Merton Parkas counted. The Lambrettas had even been on Top of the Pops, competing with the 2-Tone bands who had grown on the Mod circuit and leapfrogged their way to stardom. But there was Mod before punk, even before The Who and The Small Faces.

Rock On Records in Camden was where he liked to hang out. It was messy and packed almost to bursting point with LPs, but there were always some real gems from the 1960s for determined vinyl hunters like him. Mostly these consisted of old soul albums – Ray Charles, Aretha, James Brown, but sometimes he found something special.

Gaff gasped as he flicked past a Sam Cooke LP to uncover a pristine copy of 'Kind Of Blue' by Miles Davis. It was an iconic record for early modernists. Jazz, yes, but the very best of its kind, a reminder of the very roots of Mod, before it became mass market the first time around. He tucked the album under his arm and ploughed on in hope of discovering more gems. It took a bit of graft to plough through everything, but he had nothing else to do on a grey Friday afternoon.

Weekdays around 2pm were the best times to come here. Rock On attracted a wide breadth of street cults and there was often friction outside, particularly at weekends. But even the most determined rockabilly rebel would probably avoid a dinnertime punch-up, and at this time of day most of the Kings Cross punks were probably still lying on a piss-stained mattress in a squat with a bag of glue in their hands.

Through the window he could see loads of people hurry by into, and out of, Camden Town tube station – like little ants, intent on other people's purposes. But then Gaff spotted something more worrying – a group of unfriendly faces tumbling out from the Halfway House pub across the way. He ducked down instinctively. It was Dick Barton and his mob.

There were boxes of albums on the floor too, so Gaff pretended to be browsing intently from a crouched position.

After five minutes he gingerly stood up, just enough to peep over the stack of Stax albums that were in front of him. Fuck! Barton and his goons were just standing outside the pub waiting for something. Some of them still had the marks of the scrap on Sunday night on their ugly boats. Gaff knew that if they recognised him then retribution would be swift and merciless.

Please don't let the knuckleheads come into the shop... surely Our Price Records was more to their taste...

He took another quick look out the window and his heart dropped out of his arse. Dave was walking along the street towards Barton.

Their Dave. Mod Dave.

Luckily, he was just wearing Levi's, a Fred Perry and a green flight jacket so he didn't look overtly modernist enough to set the soul boys off on an immediate rampage. Gaff ducked down and took a deep breath. If Dave was attacked, he would have to get out there. It was suicide for sure. Six against two? Even with Dave's formidable fighting prowess, they were as fucked as a mermaid in a fish stew. But hey ho. He couldn't live with himself if a mate got done over while he cowered in hiding in the shop like a puddle on the floor.

Better to lose a few teeth than to get known as a gutless wanker.

Gaff half stood, looking down at a Booker T album, then allowed his eyes to gaze across at what he anticipated would be a scene of flying fists and bloody horror. He knew instinctively that it would have kicked off and that he would have to charge out of that door and steam into the two-bob cunts, losing the precious Miles Davis album in the process.

Except that wasn't what was happening. Dave and Barton weren't trading punches and head-butts, they were talking. Not only that there were smiles involved. Nobody was getting a dig.

Gaff moved back to the central aisle of records, so there would be a few punters in front of him, lessening the chance of any of the gang easily spotting him. His jaw dropped as he saw Barton shake Dave's hand. Then the whole lot of them turned and went into the pub. Together.

What the fuck was going on?

***

The Barge Aground was fairly lively once again with a good few faces mingling amongst the growing number of teenage tickets, younger Mod wannabees. Squire's 'Walking Down The King's Road' was blaring out and the Friday night crowd were opening up to another weekend when sleep was rarely on the agenda. Billy and Gaff had done their usual 'meet & greet' routine on entering the pub but now they had a corner table all to themselves and Dave's dodgy dealings were item one on the agenda.

'So what do you think he was up to?' asked Billy.

'Fuck knows. I thought it was going to kick off for sure, but they were more like old pals. He's an international man of mystery, ain't he?'

'International nutjob more like.'

'He won't have sold us out, that's for sure.'

'Even though we let him down while he was doing bird?'

'Never. That's not his style.'

'So what the fuck is he playing at? And when is he getting a fucking haircut.'

Gaff grinned thinly. 'I wish I knew, mate.'

He nodded half in bewilderment and half in frustration as he passed Billy a black bomber under the table.

'If I hadn't seen it with my own eyes…'

'If anyone else but you had told me…'

They both necked the speed tablets discreetly, washing them down with lager top, and scanned the room.

'Any new sorts about?'

'A couple who look about twelve, but other than that, no.'

There was a long pause before Gaff broke the ice. 'Did you hear about Evvy's brother? The one that's just come down from Jockland?'

Billy grunted. 'Steve? The sweaty Mod geezer? Chris told me they went round his flat and Dave was ready to kick the shit out of the bloke.'

'You could change unclesthe name and that sentence holds true for just about anybody. I hate to say it, but David has become a fucking liability. He'd start a fight in an empty room.'

'Chris said that the bloke was banging on the door for a laugh shouting about doing him in for shagging Evvy.'

'We're all fucked then,' laughed Gaff. 'You slipped her the goldfish as well didn't you?'

'No. I just got a gobble behind the bins near the Lyceum last summer. You remember? That Secret Affair Gig?'

'She gave me a knee trembler next to some bins up an alley in Piccadilly. Not far from Swallow Street as it goes. What's that all about? Has she got to be near a bin to get moist.'

They laughed loudly in unison. Billy wiped a tiny bit of moisture from his eye then grabbed his pint.

'Maybe it's a Jock thing.'

***

A few miles away in Canning Town, Chris was experiencing a rare evening of solitude. He hadn't fancied going down the Barge with Billy and Gaff, or going to see the Members with Debbie over in West London. They would be singing 'Solitary Confinement'; he was experiencing it...

In truth he couldn't face the prospect. As soon as Deb had mentioned it, memories of seeing the band at the Moonlight Club the previous summer flooded back. Charlotte had dragged him along to the gig with Billy and Dave in tow and it hadn't ended well. Once again it had resulted in bloodshed and had almost snuffed out their then embryonic romance.

The way his luck was, Chris worried that the Members might be jinxed, and just one more gig might have brought a premature end to his relationship with Debbie. Besides, he just couldn't stick the band, and other than 'Soho A Go-Go' he thought they were pretty shit anyway. Their 'Chelsea Nightclub', which all the Chelsea crew loved so much, was just a crap version of 'My Generation' with different words – a note for note steal, that they were too thick to realise.

A night on his Jack, a night off from Debbie was probably a good idea anyway. He could feel himself falling for her pretty heavily. He needed to slow that down, he needed to be sure.

Dave was out of the flat and even though that provided Chris with a rare moment of peace he was feeling restless so he went out into the cool night air and kicked his scooter into life. Being alone shouldn't mean being trapped indoors.

After an hour of mindless but pleasant cruising around the streets of London, Chris found himself, once again, parked under a tree in West Finchley outside the home of Charlotte's parents. He tried to convince himself that he 'just happened to be passing' but the reality was that he still had some of Charlotte's jewellery in the glove box of his Vespa so a visit to see her was always on the cards.

Maybe returning the final reminder of her time living at the flat would bring things to a distinct and tidy end. Maybe!

He tapped the large front door almost too gently, as if he wasn't sure he wanted anyone inside to actually hear him; but Charlotte appeared soon anyway. Obviously being back in the family home had done her some good as she no longer looked like the tear-stained burn-out she had been a few days before.

'Chris?' she said as if he was the last person she expected to see. 'What are you doing here?'

'I've brought your tom back,' he said quietly as he held out a small fistful of chains and rings towards her. 'You, eh… forgot to take it the other day.'

'Yeah,' she said sharply as her eyes momentarily blazed with anger. 'I think the scrubber in the towel distracted me.'

Chris was surprised at how pissed off it made him to hear her refer to Debbie so negatively. He tried to say something, but he thought better of it. Instead, he swallowed his anger, thrust the jewellery into Charlotte's hand and turned to leave.

His ex-girlfriend almost leapt out of the doorway and grabbed his shoulder.

'Chris, please don't go. Come inside for a coffee. I'm sorry.'

He turned to face her and could tell instantly that she was being sincere. The warmth of her smile would have defrosted a fridge freezer. Was it possible that she had more on her mind than a cup of Joe? Was it possible that even that thought excited him?

What was on the cards here? Friendship, reconciliation? Maybe even a shag?

Whatever it was he knew it was wrong. He was with Debbie now and things were stepping in the right direction for sure. She was the future. Charlotte was a step back. Look at her, standing there in the doorway, inviting him in… even though the stench of that creepy old fucker Halpin's bell-end was barely washed off her. What a fucking cheek.

Sticking around was a bad idea… but he went in anyway.

**

The Barge Aground was heaving and after the rush from Gaff's pill, Billy felt the need to step outside for a breath of fresh air. As he opened the front door a blast of The Chords' 'Now It's Gone' seeped out into the street and almost startled an elderly couple who were shuffling across the road. He lit a fag and sat down on one of the concrete steps that led down onto the street. As he perused the line of scooters on the street he sighed contentedly. Being where the action was always gave him a warm feeling. A pub or club full of Mods seemed to have a kind of insulating effect. Everyone together, away from the straights, the soul boys and all the other youth tribes that made life a pain in the arse. He could hear one of his favourite tracks, The Circles' 'Opening Up', getting a spin from the DJ inside so he flicked his fag end into the nearby bushes and stood up.

Just before he went in, he took a look up and down the road and contented himself that the punk mugs from the week before hadn't made a return visit. He failed to notice two spikey-haired figures who were lurking by a tree across the street and watching him intently.

**

'Have a seat,' said Charlotte, adding with a smile, 'or would you prefer a drink instead?'

'I'm not staying long,' said Chris sullenly.

Charlotte brought him a lager anyway. It was obviously one of her dads, some unpronounceable Italian gear in an ornate can. Chris cracked it open as Charlotte sat down beside him. She didn't crowd him but her knee rested only a few inches from his and the black nylon of her tights was almost within reach. As she settled into the chair her mini-skirt rode up her thighs a few inches and Chris cursed himself for being excited by the sight.

'So why are you at a loose end on a Friday night?'

'No reason. I just didn't feel like going to the Barge and with Dave staying at the flat there won't be much peace if he staggers back half-cut.'

'How did you end up with him staying there, Chris? He's a fucking pollution.'

Chris smiled to himself. Charlotte's posh voice really wasn't built for swearing.

'He's all right,' he said defensively.

'How long's he staying?'

'Not long. Just till he finds his feet.' Chris said that more in hope than certainty. In truth he had started to wonder exactly when his rowdy squatter was going to sling his resentful hook. Charlotte knew that discussing Dave was a dead end so she just sipped her glass of red wine and waited for Chris to say something. In the end the wait got too long.

'So you're not seeing *her* tonight?' she said, instantly regretting it.

'Look her name is Debbie and no I'm not seeing her tonight and it's none of your fucking business anyway.' Chris slammed the can down on the G-Plan coffee table and started to get up. Charlotte tried to grab him.

'Okay, okay, I'm sorry. Don't be so fucking touchy,' she said firmly then her tone softened. 'Please, sit down. Finish your drink. I won't mention her again.'

Chris reluctantly fell back into the seat again.

'Chris, I know it's all over okay,' she continued. 'I went off with Harold. I fucked things up and if I could change it all, if I could turn back time and make it so it never happened, I would do, but please, surely we can be at least some sort of friends. You meant a lot to me, you still do.'

'Friends? Fuck off. That's just what birds say when they want to give someone the elbow.'

'All right! How about just not enemies? It wasn't so long ago that we were lovers. I still miss it.'

I'll bet you fucking do, thought Chris, now that Halpin's ancient throbber was off the menu. He glared at her, unsure of what to say next and then he realised how sad she looked. They had shared some great times together and had barely been apart until her so-called modelling career began. They liked much the same music and she got on well with all his friends, especially when Dave was out of the way giving Her Majesty pleasure.

He also noticed how drop dead gorgeous she was looking under the subtle light of a Habitat floor lamp that probably cost half a bin man's weekly wage.

Charlotte leaned forward slightly and her lips glistened. He tried for a second to resist but his loins had taken over. He kissed her and she fell back onto the couch, pulling him with her. Their hands explored one another greedily. As her hands fumbled with his belt and zip he was sliding her tights down, stroking her thighs and lower legs all the way to the toes. Before he had dropped the hosiery, she was pulling off her panties with a flourish. Chris had only managed to pull his trousers and briefs down to just below his knees, but needs must when the devil drives. He plunged into her, and was delighted to find her wetter than the Thames in full flood. As he sank in all the way, Charlotte hands clutched his buttocks and pulled him closer, so not so much as a quarter of an inch of his manhood remained out in the cold.

They bucked wildly together, the sweat building up rapidly under all their remaining clobber. This was no tender bout of lovemaking, more an animalistic grunt and grapple session involving two people who really should have known better. Charlotte's whimpering turned into howls. She was close to her destination and getting closer, so Chris pumped away even harder. She came quickly, but he was a close second.

He let it soak for half a minute and then reluctantly withdrew. Now they were laying slightly apart on the couch, both breathing heavily. He looked at her face. She looked happy, but the smile didn't seem to go all the way to her eyes. Was she feeling regret? Was he? He didn't think so.

Should he was an entirely different question.

***

As the back lights of the last scooters melted into the mild Barking night, Billy and Gaff stood outside the Barge, swaying slightly, as Terry the landlord locked the door behind them. A few other Mods were chatting a short distance away, too full of speed to even consider turning in and going home.

'Shit,' said Billy. 'I should have gone for a piss before we left.'

He banged on the pub door. 'Tel, it's Bill. Can I pop in just to use the khazi please mate?'

The only answer he got was all the pub lights being switched off. They both walked down the street a bit but the looming Curfew Tower in front of St Margaret's Church across the Broadway offered a discretely dark opportunity that Billy could not resist.

'I'm off in there for a gypsy's,' he said desperately.

'Fuck off you heathen, that's consecrated ground,' laughed Gaff. 'You'll end up in the fires of hell.'

'Rather that than pissing in these new strides.'

Billy started to cross the road.

'I'm walking back to the Barge to do a bit of business,' yelled Gaff, thinking that the few Mod stragglers hanging about outside the pub would probably be up for a deal on the remaining little blue pills he had in his pockets.

Billy made it into the dark archway and relieved himself gleefully, gasping in relief, leaving a waterfall of warm piss cascading down the holy stonework.

The footsteps behind him took the smile off his face. Probably some aggrieved vicar. He prepared his apologies as he did up his flies and turned around, but it wasn't a man of the cloth who had caught him bang to rights. It was two punks, no doubt local yobbos, a tall muscular one and a weedy looking little bastard who spoke first.

'You dirty fucker, pissing on our manor,' he squawked. 'I thought these Mods were meant to be clean types?'

'I heard they rub talcum powder on their bollocks,' said the dopey giant who looked like a young Bernard Bresslaw from the Carry On films.

'Ah well,' said Billy in a matter of fact manner, 'If you've finished talking about my balls, I'll just be off.' He tried to walk away nonchalantly but the big punk blocked his way and pushed him roughly against the wall that he had just lubricated with urine. But fuelled by speed, Billy was fearless.

'Really Bernard? You want to play rough?'

'Look you cunt, we can do you over if you want it but that's not what we're here for.' The mentally challenged man mountain poked his finger hard against Billy's chest to accentuate every other word. He had big hands. Fucking great big Yeti ones with hairy knuckles and covered in cheap, lairy skull rings from Kensington market. Billy took a deep breath and kept his mouth shut as he sussed that a punch in the boat would probably guarantee him a visit to the dental hospital.

'That's it,' said the big punk in a hushed but menacing tone. 'You just listen and you won't get your fucking smart trousers dirty.'

The little runt sniggered loudly as he scanned around the street outside for any passers-by. Even pumped full of speed and lager, Billy knew caution was the best way to play this. Until Gaff came back, at least.

'We want a straightener with all you little Mod cunts, this Sunday at Greatfields Park. Bring as many as you fucking like but make sure you turn up.'

'What's brought all this about?' said Billy, in the tone of a politician trying to fake sincerity.

'It's about wiping you lot off the face of the earth,' piped up the smaller punk; he was bolder now and feeling like a glue-bag godfather.

'The Barge, the 100 club, the Bridge… you're like fucking ants. You get everywhere. Poofing about on your little mopeds… it's hard to tell the birds from the blokes.'

'Yeah, it must be hard for blokes like you, you don't know what sex you want to fuck first.'

The big punk leapt forward and his meaty fingers squeezed Billy's throat.

'My cousin got knocked out by one of your lot on the train this week. Spark out on a Tuesday morning. He wasn't doing fuck all and yet he said a mob of Mods done him over. You tell your friends to be there on Sunday, twelve in the afternoon.'

The punk released his grip and started to walk away.

'High noon?' muttered Billy as he stroked his aching neck. 'You've been watching too may Westerns pardner. That's it, you and Tonto can fuck off now.'

The big punk stopped in his tracks then in three quick strides he was back in front of Billy and planting the toe of his army boot into his guts. Billy collapsed to the ground and gasped loudly for a breath.

'Sunday, cunt!' echoed a voice in the darkness.

But as the punks walked away, Billy heard the big lummox ask, 'How did he know my name was Bernard?'

9

Saturday 26th of April, 1980

The street was quiet as Chris pulled his scooter up outside the entrance to his flat. It was very early in the morning and as it was a Saturday there was none of the daily business that usually filled the streets with vans, buses and armies of schoolkids trudging under duress to Rokeby School, the local comprehensive. He had not meant to spend the night at Charlotte's but whether it was fatigue, an ejaculation comedown or simply just the effects of Italian lager he had fallen asleep in her arms. Both of them had only woken when the first rays of daylight poked through the French windows leading from her parents' expansive living room into the garden. He had stayed for a coffee at least but the time between pulling his clothes back on and leaving with no more than a stilted 'Goodbye' was excruciatingly painful. He'd enjoyed it, of course he had – his slightly sore manhood testified to that. But he was also pained by an unfamiliar feeling of guilt. He'd cheated on Debbie, the girl he loved, with the girl he used to love. And if that wasn't bad enough he knew who her uncles were. If the news ever got back to her, who knows what revenge the Knights might take on the idiot who upset their favourite niece...

What had it meant to Charlotte though? Maybe it was the fuck that said fuck off for good, a couple of shags to get all the tension and unfinished business out of their systems; but he got the feeling that Charlotte wanted more though; that last night – and now his memories returned, 3am this morning – had been part one in her masterplan for the two of them to get back together.

Chris chained his scooter up in the little alley next to the bin sheds then looked up at his living room window. The light was on so he assumed Dave was in and awake. In his current emotional state, he felt that getting the third degree from his mate would probably lead to Dave denigrating Charlotte somehow and a shouting match would follow. He didn't want that.

He had his hand on the door to the front entrance of the flats but then he sighed and started to walk down the street. Gaff could always be relied on to lift his spirits.

The Arthur household smelt like a truck stop café and noise levels were rarely below deafening. Gaff had almost too many siblings to count and along with the procession of cousins and family friends that seemed to stay over regularly, it was like visiting a cross between a doss house and a travelling circus. As usual, the front door was open.

Chris walked into the hall and shouted.

'GAFF! You there, mate?'

Kids in nightwear were tumbling and stumbling past him, taking absolutely no notice of him. He tried again, and he yelled for the third time, Gaff came downstairs to join him.

'You're up with the cock,' said Gaff cheerfully.

'I was mate, that's why I'm here so early.' In reality Chris was in no mood to joke but the opportunity to crack the gag was too good to miss.

Gaff gestured to Chris to follow him through the kitchen. 'I thought the lovely Debbie was out last night,' he asked as they continued out into the garden.

'She was.'

'Oh, fuck off,' gasped Gaff as he stopped in his tracks on the worn patch of grass that passed for a back garden. 'You didn't go back to the little princess of N12 did you?'

'Am I that transparent?'

'Silly question really.'

They stopped outside a little shed at the bottom of the garden and Gaff gave its door a kick. Two figures inside leapt off the floor. One was a young geezer and the other was a girl of a similar age and they looked slightly sweaty and heavily guilty. Gaff grabbed them both and pulled them out into the garden.

'You dirty little cunt,' Gaff yelled at the boy. 'That's your cousin you little hillbilly.'

'No it's not,' yelped the kid. 'This is Auntie Rita's stepdaughter.'

'It's still family, you little moron,' growled Gaff. 'Now piss off, both of ya.'

The teenagers walked back to the house, straightening their clothes out as they went. Gaff and Chris sat down on some old milk crates in the shed.

Gaff sparked up a freshly rolled joint and took a lungful.

'We nearly got done over last night while you were playing hide the saveloy with your posho ex,' he said as he exhaled a thick plume of smoke. 'Those fucking Becontree punks are looking for a straightener this Sunday.'

'What the fuck is that all about?' groaned Chris. That was all he needed. Another mass brawl and more expensive clobber straight in the bin afterwards.

'I dunno mate. Just more of the same I suppose. It seems they want us out of the Barge. Maybe out of the way altogether. All I know is they told Billy they want us up at Greatfields Park on Sunday. High noon.' Gaff laughed when he remembered the iconic timing of the rumble.

'It's not fucking funny is it?' snapped Chris. 'We'd better get the word round to as many faces as we can tonight otherwise we are in for a right fucking pasting.'

'It might take more than that mate,' said Gaff quietly. 'There's fucking loads of those glue-sniffing bastards on that estate. It's a breeding ground for them for some reason. The only Mod geezer I know from up there was Chalky White and he got so much shit he moved in with his sister in Deptford.'

'Fuck me, it must have been bad.'

'It's a fucking jungle up there and if they bring along a load of other local herberts with them it is going to be like bleedin' *Zulu*. I think we might have to call in a few old friends.'

'Who?' asked Chris but he suspected what was coming.

'Our old football chums from last summer.'

'What makes you think the ICF is going to want anything to do with this?'

'We were with them in Wrexham and during that tear-up in Chislehurst,' reasoned Gaff. 'Surely the owe us something?'

'I don't know,' said Chris, 'Maybe.' He was not convinced but it did seem an avenue worth exploring. It might put them in debt to the ICF boys once again but it was better than getting massacred by the Becontree mob. 'They were really Dave's mates.'

'Maybe not anymore,' said Gaff almost to himself. He was about to tell Chris how he had spotted Dave getting all chummy with Dick Barton and his Gooner goons outside the boozer in Camden but then he held back.

Chris looked puzzled. Gaff changed tack. 'It's worth a try I suppose. Maybe he could give them a shout? Is he at your drum now?'

Chris nodded.

'Fair enough,' continued Gaff as he stubbed out the joint on top of an old paint can and stood up. 'Lead on brother, let us seek an audience with the unhinged high-priest of the hammer.'

***

Ronnie Childs had been a punk since year zero. At twenty-four he was something of an old-timer amongst his Becontree compadres and he kept an iron grip on the estate in between flogging speed, cashing dole cheques and slipping a length to any tasty punkettes that passed by. He had seen it all from glam rock through to pub rock and the antagonistic Ted revival, but it was punk that gripped him from the first night he wandered unexpectedly into The Vortex and got his mind blown by the Damned. After that there was nothing else for him, and when new wave came along and the music press decreed that punk was yesterday's music it pissed him off with a vengeance. But somehow Mods annoyed him more. Hundreds of the little bastards had colonised his favourite hang-outs, like the Bridge House and the Barge Aground. Right not Ronnie was looking for his Alamo.

He looked across the table at Dick Barton and his boys and wondered if they were any different. He had no time for their ridiculous clothes either. At least the Mods had a look, a uniform. These cunts looked like they were ready for a week in Benidorm. There was way too much pink and pastel for his liking. Three of them were wearing slacks! And big Black Matt standing guard in the corner of the boozer in denim dungarees and a string vest? Where was he picking up fashion tips?

Still business was business and Ronnie needed that cheap and readily available sulph that Barton specialised in. Every form of commerce requires some compromise. Barton slid a fag-packet filled with powder over the table and Ronnie returned the favour by slipping an envelope of cash in Dick's direction.

'I thought you might be giving it a miss this week?' said Ronnie quietly.

'Why the fuck would that be?' Barton sounded more pissed off with the world than he was normally.

Ronnie sighed slightly and took a long drink from the pint of lager in front of him. 'Just that I heard you lost a little capital along the way last Sunday.'

'That's all sorted now,' said Barton as he jammed the envelope into his trouser pocket. 'Business as usual now, no cash flow problems so don't you worry your pretty little head, Ronald. You'll keep getting what you need.'

Barton leaned forward in a vaguely threatening manner and lowered his voice, 'As long as you've done what we asked then everything will be fine.'

Ronnie stood up drained his glass then banged it down on the table with enough force to startle some of the pensioners in the boozer out of their stupors. He had to get out. The overpowering stench of Aramis and Blue Stratos that was emanating from Barton and his mob was starting to piss him off.

'It's all sorted,' he grunted. Ronnie grabbed his denim cut-off from the chair and made for the door.

***

Chris pushed open the door to his flat. 'Dave!' he yelled. No answer came the firm reply. Dave wasn't there, but there were dirty clothes scattered about the hallway floor. Chris sighed and picked up his post while Gaff walked past him into the living room. 'This place is like a pigsty since he moved in,' shouted Chris.

'It's worse than that brother.'

Something about Gaff's tone made Chris quicken his pace. The living room was like a disaster area. Everything that could be smashed had been. The chairs, the curtains and most of his clobber seemed to have been slashed to ribbons and what had been a prized record collection was now just shards of vinyl littered across the room. Then he saw the spray paint graffiti the length of his living room wall. Arsenal.

'Fucking Barton,' gasped Chris. 'It's got to be him.'

He half-ran into the kitchen. The old cigar tin that he had filled with Barton's money was still at the back of the grocery cupboard. The problem was it was empty.

'That's not the worst of it mate,' sighed Gaff as Chris walked back into the living room. 'You can see the door was all right, and the windows are untouched.'

'So?'

'Well look around, do you see Dave's gear anywhere?'

Chris looked at the corner where Dave had been keeping the few possessions since he'd left the clink. There was nothing there apart from a ripped pillow that looked, and probably was, stained with piss.

'I meant to tell you,' Gaff said quietly.

'Tell me what?'

The uncomfortable silence seemed to last minutes, although it was only about thirty seconds until Gaff finally spoke.

'I was up in Camden yesterday, on the hunt for old vinyl. I nearly had a panic attack when I saw Barton and his boyoes pour out of a boozer over the road. I ducked me nut, but when I looked again Dave was there, meeting up with Barton, shaking his hand and going for a pint with them.'

'Dave, Camden, Barton,' Chris said the words slowly as if he were having problems understanding them. Then his mood changed. 'And you didn't think that was news worth passing on?'

'I ain't had a chance, mate, what with you away with your birds all the time, we've barely seen you.'

'You've had all fucking morning, Gaff.'

Chris viciously booted a broken lampshade across the room. A knock on the door snapped him out of his rage. He looked over at Gaff.

'Who the fuck is that?' hissed Chris.

Gaff shrugged his shoulders.

'If its Barton's mob they ain't going to knock are they?'

Chris picked up a broken chair leg and walked over to the door. He held the make-do weapon in his right hand, undid the lock with left, and stood back poised to repel the invaders.

The door opened slowly and gently, and a familiar but unwelcome ruddy face peered down the messy hall. It was his supervisor, Alec Norton, wearing a suit that would have looked old-fashioned on his demob day when he got it. Chris let his right hand drop casually to his side and rested the chair leg against the wall.

'Christopher? Hello. I was just checking that everything was okay?'

'Come in'. The red-faced Scotsman followed Chris into the living room and looked around solemnly at the damage.

'As you can see, Mr Norton, I've had burglars.'

'I'm sorry to see this, son,' he said respectfully.

'We've only just discovered it,' said Gaff, stepping forward and shaking Norton's hand. 'You work with Chris, I take it.'

'Aye well, he works for me, actually but this…'

'What's made it worse is we've been at the hospital all morning for Chris's tests, and we've come back to this. It's a sickener.'

'That's terrible, Christopher,' said Norton. 'I don't know what this world is coming too, all the delinquents running amok. I just thought I should check up on you as we haven't heard from you for days. See if you're all right, see if you needed anything.' He gave Chris a long sideways glance. 'You look a bit rough mind.'

Chris mumbled something unintelligible.

'He's been bad, Mr?'

'Norton.'

'Like the motorbike?'

'Mebbe. But I wouldn't advise ye to try and ride me son.'

Gaff laughed politely, Chris barely seemed to notice.

'And as you can see he's a little bit away with the fairies even now,' said Gaff, adlibbing like a good'un. 'It's so very kind of you to come all this way, not many firms would do that.'

'Shell are a good company,' said Chris, snapping out of shock and going with it.

Alec Norton smiled benevolently.

'Yeah,' blurted Chris. 'I've been ill. I went to the doctors, a few times. I did ask for a sick note…'

'Ah that's my fault, Mr Norton,' said Gaff. 'Chris asked me to pick it up and drop it off at the office up near Waterloo. But I haven't had time to get up there yet. I'm Chris's cousin by the way.'

'Aye, sure son,' said Norton calmly. 'It's good to know he has family around to take care of him, and I can see now why you never phoned…' He pointed at the telephone which lay on the floor in five separate pieces. 'I knew you wouldn't let us down. I said that to Mr Cavendish on the top floor. He's a good lad I told him. Och well, I hope yer better soon son.'

He started to make for the door but then he stopped abruptly, turned and dug his hand into the pocket of his overcoat. 'Just one more thing,' he said like some kind of Jock Columbo. 'I nearly forgot tae give you this, just a bit of paperwork for ye. Nothing to worry about.'

'Cheers,' said Chris as he took the envelope. 'I'll see you on Monday.'

'Aye, aye, all the best,' said Norton then shot off down the landing stairs as if he was running for a bus.

Chris shut the door then sat down at the kitchen table next to Gaff.

'What's that?' enquired Gaff.

'Just something from work.' His tone was flat and disinterested.

'Well open it for fuck's sake. Put us out of our misery.'

'It's probably some fucking form to fill in.'

Chris ripped open the letter, read it, read it again, and then rolled it up into a ball and threw it towards where the metal bin used to be until it had been booted flat.

'Pools win?'

'It's my P45. The fucking tin tack!'

'The dirty bastard.'

Chris flung open the living room window and saw Norton crossing the road outside the flat.

'You fucking rotter,' he yelled down into the street. 'You could have just posted that, you red-faced Scottish wanker. Fuck you sideways, you fat jug-nosed Jock cunt!'

Norton stopped and thrust a V-sign in Chris's direction.

'Get it up ye, ya flash bastard,' he yelled with a broad beam cracking across his face. Then he laughed loudly and continued walking down the street.

Gaff patted Chris on the shoulder. 'I'm so sorry, mate.'

'Cheers, Gaff, but it's my fault. I gave him the ammo, and loaded the gun. Who can blame the fat little Jock for firing it?'

'Weller was right. *No corporations for the new wave sons.*'

'And you find out life isn't like that…'

'Will I see you later?'

'Well, there's nothing going to keep me here mate. Nothing.'

Chris waved Gaff off and then walked around the flat, mentally logging the damage to his property. He wasn't sure if it was the destruction of his clothes or his record collection that hurt the most. Most of his Mod finery had had been cut to ribbons – even his fucking Y-fronts and socks. It was a thorough job and the same diligence had been paid to his vinyl. He looked through the wreckage again but it was almost impossible to tell what was singles and what were albums as they had all been smashed so thoroughly and were now no more than fragments of black plastic.

For some reason his copy of The Jam's 'Setting Sons' had proved unbreakable but the surface of both sides had been gouged deeply with a knife. He looked again at the intact door and windows. No signs of break in at all. It must have been Dave who let him in and they seemed to find the cash fairly quickly as well, not surprisingly as Dave knew where abouts he kept it.

Chris realised at that moment that it wasn't the ruined clothes or the shattered records that hurt the most. It was his friend's betrayal. That treachery hit him like a punch in the solar plexus. The extent of Dave's betrayal was almost too much to take. Chris suddenly felt claustrophobic; grabbing his Harrington he made quickly for the street, phoning Charlotte was the only thing on his mind. It was not until the cool air of Canning Town hit him that he realised Debbie was actually the one he should call.

***

Chris finally found a phone box that was working and as a bonus didn't stink too badly of piss. He fumbled in his pocket for some spare change and his little black book. In reality it was only a small diary from 1977 but fuck all must have happened that year because the pages now contained the phone numbers of mates and some of the sorts who he had associated with over the years. There were some rough old boilers in there but he held on to their numbers anyway. You never knew when they would come in useful during some cold, lonely nights ahead. Any port in a storm...

The truth was, Chris's sex appeal had been on the increase ever since he had become a Mod but when it came to romance, he was fairly pessimistic about the long-term chances of any surviving, so this backup plan made some kind of sense. The close student of the book would have noted that some of the names were followed by a tier system, his own memory-jogging code rating his conquests for looks (one to ten) and bedroom performance – ranging between one star and seven. Very few rated the full seven. Although Deborah and Charlotte would almost certainly be top of the shop for very different reasons.

Snapping out of his daydream he phoned Debbie. She answered quickly and he filled her in about the state of the flat, his home phone, his job, and 'Judas' Dave.

'Are you sure? He really doesn't seem the sort of bloke to do the dirty on a pal.'

'Where is he then? And why was he hobnobbing with Barton and his mob up in Camden?'

'It looks bad superficially. But he's your mate, you said to me he was your rock. All the evidence is circumstantial.'

'Thank you Miss Marple.'

'Shall we get together? I might be able to cheer you up somehow?'

'Where do you fancy?'

'How about the Pompadours in Harold Hill? I've just got to pop over to see my uncles. They've got a place not far from there.'

'Your *uncles* uncles?'

'Yeah. They might even pop in for a pint.'

'Great,' said Chris nervously. Him and the Knights, drinking buddies? Fuck. It was only after he'd hung up that he remembered the state of his schmutta… and the uncomfortable fact that he now had no income whatsoever. A flash of inspiration hit him; he grabbed his wallet and dug deep inside. It was there! A ticket from the dry cleaners on Barking Road. What a result. Not only was it his last remaining whistle, it was one of the best – an Italian cut three-button job with ticket pocket in rich burgundy. Maybe things were looking up? He still had Debbie, he could get another job, the flat could be tidied and the damage repaired. It was not the end of the world. At least they didn't shit on the bed.

***

Chris's face fell when Debbie broke the news that they wouldn't be meeting the Knights in the Pompadours. But then she broke the better news – they would be meeting them at Uncle Steve's place in Emerson Park instead. The young Mod lovers rolled slowly through the quiet tree-lined streets of the poshest part of suburban Hornchurch on his Vespa. Many of the houses they passed were large Edwardian and Victorian villas but there were also a few huge but garish new-build houses that looked as if they had been designed by winners of the football pools that believed *Dallas* was the last word in glamour. Big gaffs worth hundreds of thousands but adorned with over-elaborate wrought-iron work, cheesy garden ornaments and glaring exterior lights. *No fucking taste at all*, thought Chris. It was the architectural equivalent of the old saying, 'all the gear, but no idea'.

Debbie knew where she was going but had an annoying habit of shouting 'turn here' just after they had passed the junction she was referring to. Then she moved on to, 'It's Yevele Way, no… hold up, Peerage Way… no Herbert Road for sure. It's near a tree.' Chris just laughed quietly and enjoyed her company. It felt good to have her holding on tightly behind him especially after the day he had experienced. Her shapely pins were warming the back of his legs and he was sure that her soft wool mini-skirt was riding way up her thighs even though he couldn't quite see round enough for a proper eyeful. His thoughts turned to their previous sexual adventures and he chucked to himself. She might have no sense of direction but she certainly knew her way around a purple helmet.

'That's the one,' yelped Debbie as she pointed at a house in the distance. Chris moved towards it, slowly at first in case she changed her mind again. A high imposing wall surrounded the property and when they got to the entrance, a geezer who could have been carved out of marble opened the heavy iron gate for them. He smiled at Debbie but said nothing as he gestured for them to park at the side of the house in between a gleaming black Jaguar XJ-S and a white Range Rover Monteverdi that looked as if it had never been through a dirty puddle in its entire existence.

The house was breath-taking; a huge bungalow with massive windows and state-of-the-art security devices set in almost an acre of well-groomed gardens. Outbuildings and garages peppered the plot and the large mahogany front door was located at the top of five wide steps.

Chris took off his helmet then stroked his suit gently trying to remove any hint of a crease. Debbie laughed quietly and tugged his hand as she bounced up the steps. The entrance to the house was slap bang in the middle of a large patio area which was covered in exotic pot plants and raised flower beds. If Steve had kidnapped a gardener from Kew, reasoned Chris, or he had really green fingers – at least when they weren't covered in blood?

Debbie had explained that as far as the books and polite society were concerned both of her uncles were entirely legit and honest taxpayers with a string to lucrative businesses including top-class West End nightclubs, a cab firm, restaurants and a building firm. For the nosey or inquisitive, the only sign of their villainous roots would be found in the criminal records of the people who worked for them. 'What can I say,' Debbie had asked with a rhetorical shrug. 'My uncles just like helping people back onto the straight and narrow.'

But odds on they would also have a penthouse flat or two for the nights when they wanted to escape the families they loved so dearly.

Debbie rattled the door heavily with her knuckles and Chris took a sharp intake of breath that he hoped she hadn't noticed. Steve Knight appeared looking dapper as ever in a casual but expensive looking shirt, some black slacks and a pair of gleaming slip-on loafers. He gave Debbie a quick cuddle, shook Chris by the hand firmly and led them into the living room.

Chris's jaw dropped open like an escape hatch, quick and wide. He tried to stop it, but couldn't quite manage it. The whole pad was stylish with a capital S. Every inch of fixtures and fittings looked immaculate... and expensive. He gawped at what appeared to be a genuine Lichtenstein on the living room wall, with a signed Dali lithograph on the wall leading through to the kitchen. The living room was bigger than his flat and had an unusual mix of levels from a dining area on a raised section of flooring to a sunken leather couch that was large enough to seat a rugby team – and their mates.

The music playing was intriguing. It sounded like sixties jazz but Chris didn't recognise it. Steve gestured to his new visitors to follow him over to a bar area where he fixed them a drink, then he walked them on to the seating area where three older men were lounging under a cloud of cigarette smoke. Chris noticed the unusual combination of laughter lines and scars.

'Chaps,' said Steve loudly enough to get their attention. 'Debbie you all know I'm sure, but this is her young man, Christopher.'

'Oi, oi,' said the oldest looking man. 'Has he got her up the duff, boss? Should I go and get that length of plastic sheeting out of the torture room?'

Chris's bottle crashed but Steve Knight only laughed loudly, along with Debbie.

'No Roy, you cheeky old cunt. My niece is still virgo intacta. Isn't that right, Deborah.'

'Whatever he said,' she said solemnly.

Knight turned back to Chris then waved his hand around the group. 'Chris, that's my brother Kenny in the suit that looks like one of Max Miller's cast-offs, my comedian mate Roy Pugh and Arthur Bennett. Now, there's a lot that I could tell you about Mr Bennett but it's not the type of thing I would care to pass through Debbie's innocent ears.'

'I've heard it all,' quipped Debbie. 'It don't bother me. Even that story about the midget and the Welsh brass.'

They all roared with laughter; Chris gave a quick chuckle so as not to feel out of it.

'You've already met Butch outside I presume?' asked Steve. 'He's not house trained yet so we've got a warm shed in the garden for him. Don't call it a Wendy House unless you really want to piss him off.'

Chris smiled. He suspected Butch was more of a lookout man, lurking in the shadows around the house fully tooled up and ready to repel borders. Not that many would dare target the Knights.

'Anyway, sit down, sit down,' Steve continued and before long Chris began to relax in their company as the drinks flowed and the more humorous tales of the previous two decades were dug up and kicked back into life.

Later in the evening Chris was making his way back from the downstairs toilet (one of three) when Steve collared him in the hallway.

'You all right, my son?' he asked warmly.

Chris nodded. Steve put his arm around his shoulder and guided him towards another door. 'Just a couple minutes in here Chris,' he said in a friendly manner, even though it still sounded more of an order than a request. They walked into a smaller room; Steve switched on the light. This was obviously a study and in stark contrast to rest of the house it could have been straight out of a Steam Smoke & Mirrors Victorian novel. Every stick of furniture was highly polished antique wood, the curtains were thick dark green drapes and the bookshelf-lined walls were creaking with leather-bound tomes. Steve sat behind a heavy 19th century desk and his ancient padded chair creaked wildly as he flopped down in it. He gestured to Chris to sit down in the chair at the front of the desk. This seat was much lower allowing Steve to glower down at him from the other side of the desk.

Chris felt uneasy, and more so when the gangster opened and shut his top desk drawer four times for no apparent reason.

'I heard you had a bit of trouble on the way back from Margate last week?'

'Yeah,' said Chris warily. 'Just some mugs on the train. You know? The usual.'

'Yes, I know son,' said Steve with a hint of a smile. 'It's always been the same. Fucking morons who can't handle someone with a bit of style. Anyway, I just wanted to say that I'm very grateful. Debbie's very dear to me. I don't like to think of anything bad happening to her.'

His tone was concern but Chris could still feel that there was a whiff of threat in there somewhere. 'Nice whistle,' said Steve as he pointed at Chris's suit. 'Have you been into all this for long?'

'A couple of years,' said Chris respectfully. It seemed longer as so much had been packed into that period. 'Once I started to hear bands like The Jam and Secret Affair that was it really… I went back into the history, the sixties and bands like the Small Faces. I also loved the look, the clobber.'

'It's a bit different from my day,' said Steve as he seemed to peer of into the distance, deep in thought. 'Endless nights in Soho clubs, shopping in Carnaby Street… I used to hit all the boutiques with a young sort called Lizzie Davies. Lovely girl, tasty too, she could have given Twiggy a run for her money.'

Steve fell silent and Chris struggled to find a way to get the conversation back on track.

'Still about, is she?' he asked.

'What? Yeah, I'm sure she's about… somewhere.' He shook his head as if to erase a memory, then he snapped back to attention. 'I think I've seen a few of these bands on the box now and again. Top of the Pops, that type of thing. I like Secret Affair and the Small Hours but most of them are just punks in suits,' he said, with a laugh. 'Where's the soul? They need a right good blast of Geno to sort them out.'

'We're still into all the original soul and blue beat,' Chris protested. 'If you came to one of our nights, you would hear The Snake and Do I Love You…'

'Yeah, yeah. I'm only pulling your chain. That's what Mod is about anyway ain't it. Evolving. Staying sharp. Look how I'm dressed now…'

Chris looked admiringly at Knight's pristine designer clothing.

'… Now to me this is smartest clobber around. Stylish. So I don't wear the Freds anymore because I'm not a museum piece. But it's the same thing ain't it? Looking good, looking *better*, leaving all the other cunts choking in our dust. No wonder they all want to take a pop at you. You outclass them. You're not a mug with a glue bag.'

Chris nodded. He felt awkward, not sure if he was being checked out or humoured, or if Uncle Steve was laying a trap for him.

'What was that music playing when we arrived, Mr Knight?'

'Please! It's Steve, Chris. Only Steve to friends of ours… and that music was the Oliver Nelson classic Blues And The Abstract Truth. One of the all time greats. You like it?'

'Yeah. I've been listening to Miles Davis a lot lately.'

'Good lad. You'll never top 'Kind Of Blue'.'

Chris had exhausted his knowledge of jazz, and just nodded dumbly. The conversation had stalled again. Steve seemed to be waiting for Chris to say something else but he didn't.

'So, you're getting on all right now, are you? No major bother about?'

Chris sheepishly mentioned the trouble he was having with Barton and his mob.

'Dick Barton? What the old fella?'

'No, it's his son.'

'Fuck me! The cunt don't fall far from the cunt-tree by the sounds of it. Him and his shit little firm of posers... Don't you worry about him, young Chris. Take it from me, that family... their luck won't last. Fucking parasites.' Steve slapped the table so loudly as he leapt to his feet that Chris almost soiled his pants. 'Come on, son, let's join the rest of them. I don't want to leave my niece too long with those fucking animals.'

***

Two hours later, Chris pulled his scooter up at a tea stand near the Woolwich ferry and within a few minutes he and Debbie were staring out over the dark waters of the Thames cradling plastic cups of what looked like coffee. It was hot and wet but that is where the likeness ended. The night sky was less murky. With the stars in the clear sky and moonlight shimmering over the Thames, it felt like a scene in a romantic film. Chris looked at Debbie – as pretty and perfect as the starlight – and thought the unthinkable. If he'd had a ring, he'd have dropped to his knees there and then.

He went to kiss her just as she turned her head away.

'Thanks for today, Deb. That was just the tonic I needed after all that's happened.'

'Yeah, I noticed the glint in your eye...' She paused and spoke quietly. 'I'm glad you got on with my uncles.'

'Fucking amazing. What a pair of geezers. Top boys. Legends!'

Debbie squeezed his arm slightly to bring him back down to earth.

'I love them both Chris. They've both always been there for me but… well, what they do, it's not for everyone.'

'What does that mean?'

'It means not everyone in their trade reaches retirement age. They've got a bit of glamour; I get that, but I've seen enough of that in my life and I don't like it.'

'You're going around the houses a bit Debs. Shall we cut the crap and get to the point?'

She looked hurt but carried on regardless. 'My point is, I think getting involved in this stupid ruck tomorrow is a waste of fucking time. It's kids' stuff, playground stuff. There's no profit in it, and no point. Rolling about with a load of thicko punks on a Sunday afternoon is not really what I look for in a bloke.'

'How can you say that, with your family tree?'

'At least my uncles get paid for what they do,' she snapped. 'Yeah, they run with the hounds, but it's made them minted. They're not just having a punch-up like a bunch of kids. Soppy gangs of mugs fighting over stupid fucking territory like packs of rats. This ain't *Quadrophenia,* you arsehole. Why have you got to be involved? You've lost your job. Your flat's a shit-hole. You need to sort your life out. What have you got to offer me, or any bird come to that?'

Chris looked perplexed. 'I can't just turn my back on it. It's gone too far. It's got to be dealt with.'

'Dealt with? This type of bother just leads to more of the same shit. Do you know what happened to me last night, Chris? I didn't want to tell you in case you went off your nut.'

'What?' The question was loaded in sarcasm.

'Me and Lizzy were making our way to Camden tube after the gig when we got stopped by four soul boys. Utter knobs obviously but they knew who I was. They were looking for you. The little one pinched Lizzy's handbag and one of them grabbed my tits and asked where they could find you.'

'Fuckin' Barton,' hissed Chris.

'I slapped him right across the dish but it's not funny Chris. I don't need this type of shit. Luckily a big black bloke had a quiet word with them and they fucked off.'

'I'll fucking do him,' seethed Chris.

Debbie turned to face him and shoved him on the shoulder. 'I don't need that. I'm looking for a boyfriend not a fucking bodyguard. You give me his name and *I'll* sort him out with one phone call. This is not what I want in a relationship, Chris. It's bollocks. You're not the big glory boy leading the charge. You're pathetic.'

The words stung. 'Well if you don't like it you can fuck right off!' he yelled, his blood boiling. Even as the words left his lips he regretted them. The effect was immediate. Time seemed to slow as he watched his perfect night crumble around him. Debbie didn't say another word. She just turned away and walked off sharply, hanging her crash helmet on the handlebar of his scooter as she went.

Chris stood rooted to the spot watching her back and wrestling wildly with his feelings. Debbie was almost the last good thing in his life but now she was walking out of it. She hadn't even given him the courtesy of a final insult. His heart was breaking but pride stung him so badly that he hesitated, like an oaf, for just too long. By the time he shouted her name and ran after her she had melted into the night. Gone.

Forever? Fuck.

10

27th of April, 1980

High noon at Greatfields Park was not as cinematic as it sounded. As the Mods filed through the small gate on Movers Lane the trees near the entrance were struggling to recover after the cold winter and only the merest touches of green adorned their branches. The tower blocks in the distance stood gloomily as a reminder that this patch of grass was simply half a dozen hectares stranded in the middle of the concrete jungle. Chris inadvertently kicked an empty can of Special Brew as he led them forward. The first bench that they passed was decorated with a pair of shit-stained Y-fronts and a discarded Durex.

'Looks like someone had a better night than you mate,' quipped Gaff drily, as he pointed at the semen-filled condom. Chris tried to laugh but the low-rent setting was more grim than funny. Maybe the thought of getting done over good and proper in the very near future had robbed him of his sense of humour.

'At least everyone's turned up,' continued Gaff as he pulled a length of bike chain out of the pocket of his Harrington. There was indeed a good number of faces from the Barge and the Bridge House; even a crew from The Wellington. There were thirty-handed, give or take, but no one was feeling buoyant. No chants of 'We are the Mods' filled the mild London overspill air.

Chris, Billy and Gaff stopped at the circular path just after the tennis court and the crowd gathered around them. As they waited, a few groups of familiar faces appeared from the direction of Greatfields Road. Chris breathed a sigh of relief. The Mod mob was growing in size. Then he heard a loud noise in the background. It was someone shouting 'Easy, easy' in a thick Scottish accent. Chris looked up and saw Lorna approaching accompanied by Evvy, her brother Stevie, and another Mod geezer who looked familiar. The stranger was well turned out with a neat black V-neck jumper over a crisp white button-down shirt and a pair of sta prest trousers with a crease sharp enough to cause criminal damage. He had come prepared too – he was swinging a pickaxe handle in his right hand.

Evvy spotted Chris, Gaff and Billy and she barged her way towards them with her group.

'What the fuck did you bring him for?' grumbled Gaff, pointing at the stranger.

Chris realised who the bloke was. Barry Morgan, top boy of the gang of skins that came from the housing estates around the Waterloo area. They had nothing but trouble from that mob whenever they went to nights out at The Wellington boozer and as they made that trip at least once a month, those tussles had been numerous. Chris hadn't seen Morgan since he and his brother Mark unexpectedly offered them some assistance against a gang of greasers at Southend one Bank Holiday weekend. They had shared a few pints afterwards but that was as far as the *entente cordiale* had lasted. He looked different now, probably having seen the error of his ways and had swapped his eighteen-hole DM boots for some tidy schmutter.

'All right lads,' he said in a vaguely friendly manner but Chris noticed his grip tightening slightly on his weapon just in case his appearance was about to cause problems.

'Fuck off, Morgan,' snapped Gaff. 'We don't need no boneheads to help us out.'

'Shut yer fuckin' mouth wee man,' roared Stevie, who moved forward quickly and poked Gaff in the chest. 'Barry's one of us, and he's a mate of mine.'

'A mate?' yelled Billy. 'You've only been down here a few days, you daft sweaty sock. Him and his brother and all his dopey mob are fucking poison.'

Stevie looked as if he was about to headbutt Billy but Barry got between them.

'All right for fuck's sake,' he yelled. 'If it's going to cause problems, I'll go but…' He paused for a moment as he glanced over Chris shoulder. '… I think you're going to need me.' They all followed his eyeline and spotted an army of punks walking up Perth Road. The procession seemed to be endless and it was obvious that the punks had swelled their numbers with local herberts and some skins from the estate, no doubt recruited on just the promise of full-scale violence.

Although the noise from the Mods was fairly muted the Becontree oiks were full of piss and vinegar, yelling loudly and chanting some vaguely audible threats.

Chris stared at the dopy Sid Vicious clones as they approached and reached for the tyre iron that was tucked into his waistband at the back of his trousers. He was properly in the mood for battle after the past few weeks. He had lost a girlfriend, found a new one, lost her as well, lost his job, lost his clothes, his records, his furniture… and so if he lost his life now, so fucking what? What did he have to live for, except for the glory of smashing these cunts into the ground?

He'd experience more highs and lows in the last ten days than most punters enjoyed in a year, all packed in to a short, speed-driven, ultraviolent period. It was knackering. The Mod lifestyle never stopped. Fashions, music, people… they all changed, evolved, at a frightening rate and you simply had to keep up or you'd be left in the dust. Time for action? It was always time for fucking action and it was exhausting him even though he loved it with a passion that he had never felt before. Everything up to becoming a Mod was just a grey smudge of old memories. No fucker was going to try and take what he had again, certainly not the approaching army of 'punks' who had learnt what little they knew about the cult from the centre spread of the fuckin' *Sun* newspaper.

From what he could see at this distance, he didn't know a single one of them, he didn't even recognise any of their ugly, leering mugs from the occasional battles at the Barge Aground. It didn't matter though… they were the enemy and they were getting done anyway.

'Fuck me,' hissed Billy, 'There's fucking loads of the cunts.'

As the punks entered the park they fanned out into a massive arc of leather-clad warriors, resplendent in their bullet belts, buckles, bleached denim and heavily-ringed fingers. Bizarrely there were a few geezers in flared jeans, army boots and denim jackets – like some pocket of bovver boys from 1976 re-animated for today's aggro.

The mob stopped a few hundred yards away from the Mods but continued with the bellowed verbals as they waved their makeshift weapons around. Bike chains, bottles, clubs and tree branches were brandished while the pale midday sun glinted off more than a few blades. Chris felt a deep, sick feeling in the pit of his stomach. The Mods were heavily outnumbered and nobody had any intention of playing it by the Marquess of Queensbury rules. He looked around. Quite a few of the Mod boys were starting to gee themselves up. They began yelling back and shuffling impatiently from side to side.

Even though the odds were against them there was no way out now and tension was growing unbearable for many.

'Chris,' snapped Gaff. 'Behind us mate, look…'

Chris turned to see a large, boisterous gang approaching from the rear. For a second he thought it could be a pincer movement, trapping the Mod force between too brutal claws. They would have to form a circle, and defend attacks from all sides. He opened his mouth to bark his orders, but then he realised the newly arrived hoolies were showing no sign of aggression towards them. They actually walked past the Mods and began lining up at the front. These faces he did recognise. It was West Ham, a thirty strong mob of hardcore ICF hooligans headed up by the ex-glory boys Mickey Thomson and Terry Harkins. Real tough fuckers. They looked as focused at paras, glaring straight ahead at the enemy.

Although their appearance was unexpected, it was obvious whose side they were on. Terry looked over at Chris insolently and shrugged his shoulders.

'What are you fucking waiting for?' he shouted.

Chris was about to reply, but then he heard a roar from Evvy's brother behind him.

'Get intae thae fuckin' bastards.'

The fight began. The two opposing sides came together so solidly that initially there was hardly any room for anyone to move. It was like a Monday morning scrum on the tube but one where each commuter was trying to slash or kick the other. Gradually victims were chosen and the melee spread out into a myriad of smaller confrontations. That was where the real damage was done. The ICF lads seemed to have some sort of gameplan that involved taking out all of the biggest punks as soon as possible, unnerving some of the others as their top boys bit the dust. Billy caught a glimpse of the moron that had cornered him outside the Barge and managed to kick his knee in and follow through to land a knockout right on the big mug's face before a short, spotty punk tugged him down by his skinny tie and a flurry of fists dropped him to the floor. Gaff was yelling obscenities somewhere in the distance,

Barry Morgan and Stevie the Sweaty Sock had initially laid waste to more than a fair few two-bob 'anarchy' merchants but exhaustion was now setting in.

'How many of these cunts do we have to knock out?' shouted Barry.

'Och, only another thousand or so.'

Tiredness hadn't reached Chris yet. Bobbing and weaving like a boxer, he saw the little runt from the Barton firm to his left.

'Oi, Dopey! Oi, dwarf!' he hollered. The short man's scowl was replaced by sheer rage. Too late. Chris pulled back his right arm and hit him straight in the face. He punched him so hard he seemed to lift him off his feet before he fell flat out on the grass. Chris kept going, lashing out at will. All the anger that had built up in him flowed out of him in an orgy of violence.

Despite their best efforts, the Mods were too outnumbered to make ground. Chris saw friends and faces falling to the ground all around him. Boots were going into them mercilessly. But then he spotted another group on the fringes of the park moving swiftly towards them. Back up? No chance. As they grew closer he could see it was Dick Barton and the rest of his mob, minus their big black mate, accompanied by a large group of angry looking terrace boys in tracksuits and trainers. Worse still, Dave was right there amongst them and dressed in current terrace sportswear. He looked more like he was heading to a tennis match than a vicious, street-fighting rumble. That wasn't a tennis racket in his hand though, it was his trusty hammer. As he got nearer, Chris noticed his pupils were the size of pin-pricks. His ex-pal was out of his nut on speed.

Chris gave the punk in front of him a vicious back-hand slap and charged forward towards his erstwhile mate. In his blind fury he failed to notice that Dick Barton was closer, between them to his left. Chris felt a sting. The angry Gooner had taken a wild swipe at him with a Stanley knife, catching him right on the hairline of his forehead. The pain was instant, cold and sharp, but momentum kept Chris going. He barged into Barton with his left shoulder, sending them both crashing down to the ground. Sitting astride him, Chris managed to land a few solid belts on Barton's jaw but his mob were like worker ants protecting their queen and they quickly dragged him off. Chris was thrown to the floor for a thorough going over. He curled into a ball as the hail of kicks and punches found their target. But then Stevie the Jock stepped forward swinging a captured bike chain and beating them all back. Staggering to his feet, Chris could see Dave tearing into some Mods, geezers he had spent the past year with yet now being subjected to his hammer blows. Then Stevie made a beeline for Dave. This was going to be the street cult equivalent of the Rumble In The Jungle. Shame he didn't have time to watch it.

Barton had recovered to his left, and Chris noticed through his blood-stained eyes, that the mobster's son was moving back towards him with his Stanley knife still in his grip. Barton's gaze was a mixture of emotions – smug, predatory, half-crazy. This wasn't going to be easy, thought Chris. As he steeled himself for the one-sided fight, the sounds of battle swirled all around him – yells, thuds, screams of pain. But then the bright revving sound of car engines cut through it all. Something was coming towards them. Ambulances? The Old Bill? Some short-sighted old bastard in an ice cream van?

None of the above. A gleaming Jaguar XJ-S skidded to a halt on the grass about thirty feet away from the melee with three black Bedford vans close behind it. The doors of the van flew open and a mob of hard-faced old cons jumped out, all in their thirties and forties and all tooled up.

The Knights! Steve and Kenny emerged from the Jag looking smart and unflustered, but still armed and ready for action. They almost walked over to the action. Even this calm act of aggression was enough to persuade some of the jacket-holders at the back to fuck off back to Becontree. These were geezers – grown men, the sort who pulled off armed robberies and worked doors in their spare time. Pain was what they dished out for a living. This wasn't ruck'n'roll anymore. It was payback time.

An uneasy calm settled over most of the younger fighters as the men approached. The absence of any unnecessary posturing, chanting or hand gesturing was massively unnerving for many. They seemed to just walk through the increasingly battered Mods and hit their Becontree opponents like a straight line of infantry men. Wallop! As their coshes, clubs and tools met the punks and Gooners, a wave of bodies hit the deck, followed by more kids who just hadn't scarpered fast enough.

The Knight clan just kept on moving, striking, slashing and pummelling as they went, and for most of the opposing mob it was just too much. Yet more had it off on their toes – the ones that could still walk at least. Barton yelped out some kind of rallying cry and ran towards the older gangsters but with only his small group of acolytes behind him they were soon surrounded by the Knight's firm. Only their cries of pain illustrated the horrors that rained down upon them.

With the Mods and ICF chaps now in the majority once again, some scuffles persisted but very few of the opposition had the energy or inclination to keep things going. They retreated in packs, the bolder few chanting indecipherable insults and half-hearted chants of CAL as they moved away fast. So it was true, thought Chris as he tried to stem the blood from his forehead that was still dripping down over his nose and top lip – these mixed-up losers really did support Chelsea, Arsenal and Liverpool. How did they work? He didn't get a chance to think it through. Unfortunately for him one of the retreating Becontree punks had a last gasp of energy and, yelling 'Chaos' as he ran past, he slammed whatever weapon he was carrying into the back of Chris's head.

Lights out. Chris struggled to get his eyes back into focus. Whatever he had been hit with had done the job good and proper as he could barely feel his legs. As he stared up at the fuzzy light-blue sky a flash of fear gripped him tightly in the stomach. Maybe the blow to the back of the head would cause lasting damage. Try getting on a PX125 with a fucking Zimmer frame, maybe he'd been left a raspberry? He calmed down a little as some feeling returned to his feet then he noticed Mickey Thomson, Terry Harkins and a few other ICF geezers looming over him. He still half expected a kick in the bollocks but Harkins offered an outstretched hand and pulled him to his feet.

'That's one pair of strides that won't see the light of day again,' laughed Harkins as he pointed down at Chris's ripped and muddy trousers.

'Cheers Terry,' said Chris hazily. He noticed that he wasn't the only one who had been left on his arse. In the distance some punks and soul boys were limping away and a few others were being carried. By now some Sunday walkers, pensioners and young families were creeping around the edges of the park casting a wary eye over what had recently been a battlefield.

'What are you lot doing here?'

'Those fucking Gooners couldn't keep their traps shut,' laughed Mickey. 'Once we heard they were planning to make an appearance we thought we'd offer a little assistance.'

'Yeah,' agreed Terry with a smile. 'You helped us out last year in Wrexham and we don't forget a favour. You were bleedin' useless, but at least you didn't bottle it. And you are West Ham after all. We couldn't let Arsenal invade East London and get away with it.'

'Fuck all else to do on a Sunday afternoon anyway,' quipped Mickey. 'It's good training innit?'

Terry was looking over Chris shoulder and his smile suddenly faded. 'Anyway, we'll catch you later mate. Stay lucky.' The ICF mob moved off fairly quickly and as Chris turned to watch them, he noticed Steve Knight walking towards him. As the gangster nodded curtly at the departing ICF boys Chris noticed what looked very much like Barton Dick being bundled into one of the vans.

'You all right, Chris?' asked Steve as he brushed an almost miniscule speck off mud off his brown suede sports coat. He looked almost untouched other than a few smears of someone else's blood across his knuckles. His fawn Lyle & Scott polo neck looked as if it was just out of the wrapper.

'Yeah, sure… Steve,' said Chris.

'I can tell you're not. How many fingers am I holding up?'

'Erh, two?'

'One, you doughnut. You've either got concussion or the cunts just knocked you into the middle of next week.'

'Why, ah, how, ah, why are you here Mr... Steve?'

'Do you think I'll ever forget what it is to be a Mod, son?' Steve said quietly as he gave Chris's shoulder a small squeeze. 'That feeling that you're just that bit better than all the other mugs. Knowing you've got style, sus... that feeling never leaves you. This ain't just a passing phase Chris. If you're truly into this then it's for life. That's it, you've got no fucking choice.' He smiled as he gestured to where the Becontree and Arsenal mobs had melted away into the distance. 'And all this shit, it is never going to stop because there will always be some trendy bastard that has hitched a ride on the latest bandwagon and wants to take a pop at you for sticking to your guns.'

Steve slapped Chris on the back and started to walk away. 'Keep the faith, son, and keep your guard up.'

Then he stopped just before he got back into his Jag and shouted, 'Remember, if it ever gets a bit too heavy you know where to find me.'

Chris was still standing in the same spot as the Knights' convoy drove off into the distance.

***

Chris trudged along the streets feeling a strange mix of pride and despair. Almost every part of his body ached. He found Billy and Gaff loitering outside an off licence, slurping cider.

'What's this? Victory drinks?'

Both of them looked rough. 'You need to get home and cleaned up, you look like you've just pissed off the SAS.'

'That was hell,' said Gaff weakly.

'The heaviest ruck I've ever been in,' muttered Billy. 'Fuck knows what would have happened if the Knights hadn't rocked up to even up the odds. Was that down to you?'

'I reckon. I didn't know they were coming, but they knew it had been called on.'

'We'd be leaving on stretchers... if we were lucky.'

'Shitting hell. You wouldn't mess with them.'

'The good thing is we've established a precedent,' said Gaff. 'Fuck with the Mods and you will get fucked, with extreme prejudice. Here, Chris, have a tin.'

They walked to where they had parked their scooters, some way from the battleground. Chris stayed behind to buy sausage and chips. As the area got busier, he noticed he was getting funny looks from slightly alarmed pedestrians who gave him a wide berth. When he caught sight of himself in a shop window he realised why. What had been a crisp white Fred Perry was now smeared with mud, grass stains and blood. And his Levis and desert boots were in a similar state.

He corrected his slouching posture and lifted up his chin a little. It had been a decisive victory for the Mods, and they'd all paid a price. On the plus side, it looked like Barton would no longer pose any problems and getting the backing of the Knight brothers... well, that was something else entirely. Maybe now things would calm down a bit and they could get back to the most important things in the modernist lifestyle – the music and looking good. He wasn't so sure about the women. Where did he stand with Debbie now that this was all over? How did he feel about Charlotte? She was still haunting his dreams, her memory hanging around like a bad smell in a pretty package.

Arriving home, twenty minutes later, he noticed a familiar face hanging around the corner leading to

Beckton Road. His heart sank. It was Dave. His ex-friend was in an even worse state than he was. He looked as if he had been battered, dragged through a hedge then battered again. Chris steeled himself for another confrontation.

'It's all right, I'm not here for bovver,' Dave said and raised his hands in a gesture of surrender.

For you Davey ze war ist over, thought Chris with a slight sense of relief.

'I left something at your flat. Please, just let me pick it up and I'll be on my way.'

'All you left there was fucking destruction mate. You think I'm going to invite you in after you let those mugs in to run rampant? Have a fucking word with yourself.'

Dave stared at the ground silently. He looked beaten, but you never knew where you were with a psycho. Dave sighed, 'Please Chris, it's important.' Chris let out an exasperated gasp and gave Dave a slight nod as he walked off to the flat.

***

The railway arch workshop shook with the combined noise of the heavy metal door slamming shut and the 1.15 to Victoria passing overhead. Dick Barton cursed quietly under his breath then whimpered slightly and tried to free himself from the thick insulation tape that secured his hands and feet onto a rusty metal chair. A semicircle of Knight brothers and their associates stood in front of him. Steve flicked his antique brass Zippo into action four times then put it back in his pocket.

'I bet you didn't see your Sunday panning out like this did you, Ken?' he said to his brother.

Kenny laughed and wiped a little more blood off his knuckles with a silk handkerchief. 'The last time I had a tear-up in Barking on a Sunday afternoon Joan Sims was still a dolly bird.'

'Please, Mister Knight…' pleaded Barton.

Steve raised a single finger that shut Barton up.

'You don't get to speak, son. You get to listen. Save your breath cos if I hear anything from you like 'Do you know who my dad is' or 'I didn't do nuffink' I will have your foreskin off with a pair of pliers.'

Barton gave off a low hiss that sounded like a beach ball deflating.

'I know who your fucking dad is and if he has any problem with what happened today he can speak to me, or Kenny, or any one of our colleagues here and we will straighten him out. Right out!'

Steve's final outburst echoed loudly around the crumbling brickwork of the archway. He sat on the edge of an ancient workbench close to Barton and spoke more quietly. 'You're a lot like your dad. He never listened to anything I told him and he never gave me anything but trouble and you, my son, you seem to be just the same. Everyone knows that I simply don't allow anyone else to flog pills and powders in my clubs up West. It's like, a kind of quality control system. If they are in my clubs. they get my gear. The good stuff, not snide shit brought through the doors by little cowsons like you.'

'But Mr Knight, I never…'

Whack! Steve slapped him across the back of the head, stood up and pulled out his Zippo again. It was sparked into action again four times then slid back into his pocket.

'You see, I didn't bring you here to get some kind of confession out of you,' he carried on. 'I know what the fuck you've been up to. I trust the word of my friends and one of my friends has kept me well informed.' Steve turned towards a little office cubicle at the far side of the unit and shouted. 'Matthew my old mucker, come and join us.' Black Matt appeared from the office. Barton's mouth fell open. It was Matt, his Matt, but his soul boy gear was long gone and it had been replaced with a very smart, but sober, suit with a double-breasted jacket.

'Matt?' hissed Barton. 'You work for him? You black ba…'

Steve slapped the racial slur straight out of Barton's mouth. Then he grabbed Barton by the throat and squeezed.

'You really are a nasty little shit aren't you, son.'

He let go of his grip and smiled merrily as he walked towards the door.

'I think we will leave you and Matt to get reacquainted again. Shall we go gentlemen?'

The Knights and their mob walked out of the unit laughing and slammed the door behind them. Matt took off his jacket, laid it down carefully then started to roll up the sleeves of his Armani shirt.

'Nothing personal, Dick, just business,' he said quietly as he picked up a rusty crowbar from the workbench.

***

Chris and Dave sat across from each other on the tiny gateleg table in the kitchen. The flat still looked like a hovel after Barton's spot of furniture demolition. Chris sipped his coffee but the one he had made for his guest was steaming quietly on its own as Dave stared aimlessly out of the window.

'Well?' said Chris. 'What did you come for?'

'Eh?' said Dave as he snapped out of his trance.

'You said you left something,' said Chris impatiently. 'You seemed to clear out all your gear before you set your new mates on all my stuff.'

Dave stood up sheepishly and walked over to the window in the living room. 'It's just this,' he said and waved a small photograph which had been jammed between two empty bottles on the window ledge. 'It's my mum. The only one I have. I wanted to take it to the new place.'

Chris had always seen Dave as the strong one, the lionheart. Yet the man in front of him now was a sadder, beaten figure. He could still do damage of course, but seeing his old mate standing in the wrecked living room clutching his one family snap showed how much prison had changed him. How much of himself he'd lost. Chris felt a tinge of sympathy, but then he remembered why his drum was so fucked-up in the first place.

'You got somewhere to go have you?' he asked coldly.

'Yeah, the parole board got me in some hostel up near Camden,' answered Dave. 'It's just a room but…' his words trailed off into despair.

Chris exhaled through his nose angrily, and slurped down the rest of his coffee.

'What got into you, Dave? Nine months inside and you have had the Mod hammered out of you. What are you now? A football herbert? A casual? Why have you turned your back on what we had?'

'Mod's had its day, it's not going to last,' said Dave, slightly more animated now. 'Mod's over mate, can't you see that? Fucking 2-tone is getting bigger and soppy cunts with dressing-up boxes are drifting down to Blitz. They look like something out of Carry On Dick! All of this stuff, it's temporary. You're trying to hang on to someone else's yesterday. I wanna be part of something that lasts, something now. What I am now is what I've always been, working class, English and proud. Yes, we fight at football but so what? Rucking on the terraces has been going on since Charlie Chaplin was in nappies.

There's no room for posers at football. It ain't ever gonna stop, it's going to get bigger and I want to be a part of it. This Mod thing… it's been a laugh but it's gone. It's just something for the plastics, prick-teasing tarts and the fucking scene chasers now.'

'Bollocks!' spat Chris. 'It might change or develop in some way but we're just getting started. I can't believe I'm going to wake up one morning and think, "That's it, I'm done with this, where's me spandex?". You've got it wrong mate. They must have been putting something in your porridge when you were in the boob.'

Dave just shrugged. 'I dunno. For me it's over. I think I might stick with the Arsenal lot and see what's what.'

'Piss off,' you're from Canning Town. How's that going to work?'

'My nan lives on the Westbourne Estate.'

'You're be a turncoat. How will Swallow and Cass be? You'll be the ICF's number one target. And as soon as your new mates find out you were webbed up with Mickey Thomson, Terry Harkins and all that lot you'll be fucked… at both ends probably. The ICF ain't going to welcome you back either. You squared up against 'em today with a load of soppy punks and Gooners.'

'If Barton's out of the way there might be an opening.'

'Joining that lot is not some kind of career path, Dave, it's just a bad fucking idea.'

Chris's words trailed off and a fog of silence filled the room. Dave stared blankly at the floor. Then Chris finally spoke.

'Look, you need to think things through. Gaff and Billy might take a little time to come around but we are still your mates, despite all this.' He gestured towards the wreckage around them.

Dave seemed to snap out of his trance. He pulled a wad of bank notes from the inside pocket of his pilot jacket and slapped them down on the table. It was Barton's chunk of speed money, back again like a dirty cash boomerang.

Chris laughed. 'You fucking nutter! You want to get back in with that Arsenal mob and the first thing you do is half-inch their drug money. Are you fucking serious?'

'They've got a little lock-up in Islington. I was in there yesterday and when they nipped out for a fag I had a shufty in Barton's desk. Boom, there it was. I couldn't resist it.'

Chris shook his head. But then he thought *why the fuck not* and picked up the cash.

'Thanks Dave. Look mate, I can't let all this go,' – he gestured around the damaged room, 'but get away and think things through. This Gooners idea is a bad one. A seriously bad one. Get yourself sorted in this new gaff and take some time. You've only been out the nick for less than a week and already it's been one fucking disaster after another. You need to slow down, and think what you really want to do with your life. What's best for you.'

'I know. It's just things move so fast these days. This Mod scene… it's one hundred miles an hour. At least the football thing is only every weekend.'

'What? Stop the ride I want to get off? That's bollocks mate and you know it. You're speeding through your days more than any of us. Just take a breather for fuck's sake and get your head straight.'

'Maybe.'

Dave got up and walked towards the door but paused just as he was about to leave and waved his hand around the wreckage of the room in a small arc.

'All this, mate, I'm sorry,' he said with a shrug and then he was gone.

Epilogue Part 1

One week later, Chris got back from a soul weekender in Lowestoft to find the door of his flat open. Not a-fucking-gain. He pushed it open only to find the whole place had been restored. No, not just restored, transformed. The furniture had been replenished, the walls had been freshly painted... it looked like something out of the Ideal Home Exhibition. Then things got weirder. The Knights were in his kitchen.

Steve gave him a funny look. 'You've got to do something about this coffee, son,' he said, pouring half a cup of sludge down the sink. 'It tastes like it's been sucked out of an Arab's jockstrap.'

'Mr Knight... Steve, Kenny. What the...?'

'What this? The boys done it for you. A little present from the firm. We can't have one of our own living like a fucking tramp, can we?'

One of our own? What did he mean?

'Oh and look, Chris, are you still looking for a job?'

'Yeah,' he replied dumb-plussed.

Steve produced a business card and handed it to Chris.

'This is my mate, Bish, he's in the music game – PR, management, all that shit. He's got an office in Soho, and he needs a keen young kid to run errands for him, check out new bands, that kind of shit... Does that appeal?'

'Not half.'

'Get up there today. He'll be expecting you. Wear that good whistle.'

'I... I... I can't thank you enough.' Chris was on the verge of tears.

'Don't thank us. There's only one thing I need you to do for him, and that's phone up my niece, and eat some humble pie. Give her the old fanny, but make her happy again, because she's been as miserable as fucking sin these last few days'

Epilogue Part 2

Chris sat across the table from Debbie and sipped his cappuccino quietly. It was still fairly early in the year for parasols so he was free to soak up the gentle Parisian sunlight at their outdoor table. Even though he was only 280 miles from Canning Town, the French capital seemed considerably warmer. They sat relaxing in a café terrace just beyond the shadow of the Grande Arche in La Défense. The tourist-trapping centre of Paris was not for him and he preferred the striking modernism of the city's business district.

He felt an overall sense of wellbeing, despite still recovering from the battle of Greatfields weeks earlier. Maybe it was just the surroundings… and the company. Debbie looked very chic in her tight black crew-neck knitwear and houndstooth mini-skirt, so much so that a few passing French geezers were less than subtle as they gave her the once over. Strangely he felt no immediate desire to tell them to fuck off but that may just have been the result of the relaxed atmosphere or perhaps because all his aches and pains were still relatively fresh.

Chris drained his cup then caught the waiter's attention. 'Deux cafés s'il vous plait.'

'No problem pal,' muttered the waiter in a broad Glasgow accent as he darted back inside the restaurant. For fuck's sake, a fucking Jock! The accent immediately brought back bad memories of Norton's smug face. Thanks to that bastard, he'd be up shit creek right now if it hadn't been for Steve Knight's offer. Chris calculated he would have run out of redundancy dough and the speed cash in a couple of months. He could have ended up waiting on tables to get by. He would have had to take any job going – there was no place for any self-respecting Mods on the dole. That was for punks, skins and Hawkwind fans.

Thanks to Knight, he was due to start work as soon as they got home. And in Soho! The music industry! With all the buzz and glamour... He didn't mind starting at the bottom because then, that way, the only way was up. Maybe tomorrow he'd be rubbing shoulders with Paul Weller and Ray Davies. Or getting pally with Debbie Harry. Why the fuck not? Life was looking up. He had his Debbie, he had Paris and back home he could soon have the world at his feet. Let some over mug push trolleys for Shell. Chris Davis's future was unwritten! And unblemished.

Well mostly. Charlotte had caught him at the flat just before he left to meet Debbie. She had quite a bombshell to drop too. She was up the duff. He hadn't had time to discuss whether the baby was likely to be his or Halpin's, and as his initial reaction had been less than ecstatic Charlotte had burst into tears and run off. That was one mess he'd have to sort out quickly without Deb getting a hint of it. What a palaver! Never a dull moment, eh? He smiled at Debbie and she beamed back at him. Chris stretched back in his seat and let himself bask in the sunlight as Secret Affair song lyrics flashed through his mind.

'This is my world today, and I couldn't have it any other way.'

My world? Too fucking right it is!

THE END

The Knight brothers are used in this book by courtesy of their creator Garry Bushell. You can read their origin story in All or Nothing by Garry Bushell with Craig Brackenridge.

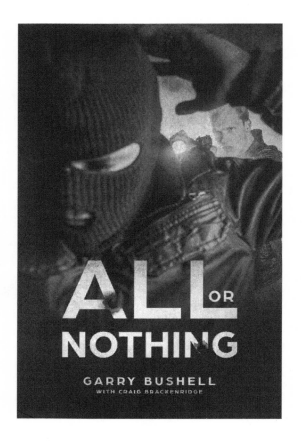